BE A LIGHT: MIRACLES AT MEDJUGORJE

BE A LIGHT: MIRACLES AT MEDJUGORJE

The incredible story of the Marian apparitions in Yugoslavia.

ANN MARIE HANCOCK

THE DONNING COMPANY
PUBLISHERS
NORFOLK/VIRGINIA BEACH

To My Love . . . my
husband of twenty years . . . Tommy
And to my beautiful children
Cori, Faith and Chip
To all the children of the world. . . .
Isn't that all of us?

Contents

In the beginning was the Word:
the Word was with God;
and the Word was God
He was in the beginning with God.
All things were made through Him,
and without him was made nothing
that has been made.
In him was life, and the life was
the light of men.
And the light shines in darkness;
and the darkness grasped it not.

John 1:1-1;5

"We cannot live without love
if we do not experience it
And make it our own, and if we
do not participate intimately in it,
our life is meaningless.
Without love we remain incomprehensible
to ourselves."

The Pope in America
San Francisco, 1987
Pope John Paul

Acknowledgments

There has been an incredible support team for this book. I owe them all much.

Bonnie Ruder, my "mentor," who encouraged me daily to write, write, write, Candy Hopewell, the principal of Blessed Sacrament High School in Powhatan, Virginia, and my sister, Pamela, who has accompanied me on numerous speaking engagements, and has been a source of constant support.

Special appreciation is extended to Martha Uzel, Cathy Vanderhoff, Linda Osby, and B. J. Curtis, the fantastic secretaries in my husband's law firm of Crews and Hancock. Their endless patience with my handwriting and excellent typing skills helped make this effort possible.

I would especially like to thank Sheri Parks, my dear friend, for her kind words, her warmth and inspiration, as well as her exceptional ability to wade through this poor author's "year of manuscripts, personal tapes, and notes." I thank Sheri and Chris Dill for their help in editing and sorting through my boxes of transcripts. I love you both.

What can I say to my family for their support of and belief in me? For the endless supply of hugs and kisses, even when they had to do their own laundry and fix their own school lunches in my absence?

What can I say to my precious Tommy, who ran my carpools in addition to all his business enterprises and substituted as "mom" in my absence? Words are inadequate. I love you more than I can express!

I also extend sincere gratitude to Manuel Loupassi—who has been so loving to my family and to me.

To the late Father Val. I love you and will always remember you. I know you are with God. You will always be a source of inspiration to me.

. . . And to Bob Friedman, my publisher, who believed in this effort, and believed in me.

I will always be grateful.

God bless you all,
Ann Marie Hancock

AUSTRIA

HUNGARY

ROMANIA

SLOVENIA
Ljubljana

Zagreb

VOJVODINA

Trieste

CROATIA

Novi Sad

Rijeko

Savo

Danube

BOSNIA
HERCEGOVINA

BELGRADE

Drina

Sarajevo

Split

SERBIA

Morova

Citluk

Mostar

MONTENEGRO

Pristina

BULGARIA

Dubrovnik

Titograd

KOSOVO

ADRIATIC SEA

Skopie

Vardar

ALBANIA

MACEDONIA

ITALY

GREECE

MOSTAR

Ljubuski

Citluk

MEDJUGORJE

Neretva

Capljina

MEDITERRANEAN SEA

Metkovic

10

Introduction

Dear Friends,

I have not, previous to this moment, been a writer. I have been a television personality and interviewer for twenty years, with an academic background in debate and argumentation. If I had to label myself, I would, with much pride, identify myself first as a wife and mother, with my family as the focal point in my life, and source of my greatest joy.

I have elected to write my personal story and experiences of Medjugorje (pronounced Med-joo-gore-ee-ae), Yugoslavia, because of my deep love of, and personal devotion to, the Holy Family, a model for us all. I also wish to share the peace I found in this holy place. I write with much difficulty, only because of the frustrations and mechanical techniques involved in the art, but I write with total conviction and determination that my experience might offer the hope, peace, and joy that Medjugorje gave me, and still offers the world.

I also write with an urgency the Holy Mother has conveyed in her messages, that time is running out and we all need to return our lives to God. We, it would seem, have separated *ourselves* from God, through our lack of understanding, and therefore shifted our focus from God to a preoccupation with materialism. Often, we are unconscious . . . unaware. What are our priorities? Televisions have become babysitters, the suicide rate among the young is at an all time high, drug use and alcoholism are common and spreading like cancer. Reports of violence and crimes fill the news media, along with broken families and broken homes. The threat of nuclear war hangs over our heads like a dark cloud.

It is time to wake up . . . for the sleeper to awaken, the dreamer to live the dream.

I am still amazed at most responses to my trip to Yugoslavia. When asked "Why Yugoslavia?" I explain that the Holy Mother has been appearing to six children for six years, attempting to guide them (and us), through Her daily messages, back to God. Comments like, "Isn't that special?" or "Why didn't you go to Bermuda or Cancun?" or,

"Sometime you must show me your pictures. Did you have fun?" stopped me in my tracks! I wondered if perhaps I was heard incorrectly. What has happened in these people's lives to elicit such shallow responses? Have they lost their spiritual focus, or is it lying dormant, just waiting for the sleeping soul to awaken? Sometimes I wonder if the whole of humanity is in a coma? Or had I crossed that fine line between sanity and insanity? I know there are those, as I was myself, yearning for deeper meaning and something more in their lives. There have to be others searching for the answer to some very profound questions of the heart: Why am I here? Where is the hope, peace, and joy in a suffering world of violence and despair? Can I make a difference? What can I do?

And so, I write this with the love, peace, and joy in my heart which was reawakened in me, in Medjugorje. I write with hope that you, too, may find those same feelings that have always been inside each one of us; that they might be stirred to fill our lives with love and concern for our own souls, and thus our fellow man.

It is my hope that you will read this book, not to accept or reject my observations and experiences, but to formulate some questions of your own (with *your* own subsequent answers), that will ultimately lead you to a simple, peaceful, and meaningful life that will become a constant joy and source of love for *you.*

We all, I believe, have a common desire in our lives. We constantly strive for peace, love, and joy, often to no avail. In these stressful times, I have found in the Holy Mother's messages, that love, that peace, that joy, are our inheritance, if we will only look within our hearts.

Ann Marie Hancock

P.S. I have included a question and response section at the end of each chapter. These questions are usually asked at my lectures about my experiences in Medjugorje. The responses reflect my own personal opinions and feelings.

Chapter 1

MEDJUGORJE:
The Village . . . the People

The Wizard of Oz
On Dorothy's returning to Kansas . . .

Dorothy: Oh, will you help me, can you help me?

Good Witch: You don't need to be helped any longer. You've always had the power to go back to Kansas.

Dorothy: I have?!?

Scarecrow: Then why didn't you tell her before?

Good Witch: Because she wouldn't have believed me. She had to learn it for herself.

Scarecrow: What have you learned?

Dorothy: Well . . . I think that it wasn't enough to want to see Uncle Henry and Auntie Em—and it's that if I ever go looking for my heart's desire again, I won't look any further than my own back yard, because if it isn't there, I never really lost it to begin with. Is that right?

Good Witch: That's all it is.

Scarecrow: But that's so easy! I should have thought of it for you!

Tin Man: I should have felt it in my heart!

Good Witch: No, she had to find it out herself.

The events which led to my visit to Medjugorje are not only interesting themselves, but are threads of the whole fabric of my transforming experience. It all began with Jackie Bailey, a dear friend of mine, who for many years has shared a tradition with me at Christmas. We exchange Christmas, and birthday, gifts (my birthday being December 26th).

Jackie came to see me at my home on my birthday, December 26, 1986. We chatted for awhile, and then she suggested that we exchange gifts. I noticed that she brought three boxes. She said that one of them was for me from her husband, Jim. I thought to myself that a gift from him was unusual as he had never been a part of the gift exchange between Jackie and myself. I was moved that he had remembered me, and very curious to see what was in the tiny white box. I opened it to find a beautiful white-beaded rosary with a silver chain. There was a small gold card at the bottom of the box which read, "Ann Marie, if you can believe in miracles, this rosary carries the special blessings of The Holy Madonna—Happy Birthday, Jim."

I was very touched by such a personal and special gift, especially the gift of the rosary itself, during the holiday season, which blesses and honors Christ, the Madonna, and the Holy Family. Jackie herself was moved by my reaction, and went on to explain the gift from her husband.

Jim had been an agnostic since I had known him. I couldn't help but wonder what it was that had inspired him to give me such a "religious" gift, with specifically Catholic connotations. What had happened to him since the last time we had visited, which had not been so very long ago?

Jim Bailey is a hard-core investigative reporter, a member of the news team of a New Orleans television station. Jackie began to explain. Jim had been asked to do a documentary with another reporter (who happened to be Catholic) on the phenomena taking place in Medjugorje, Yugoslavia. The producer felt that Jim, given his agnostic background, would assume the position of "the doubter," thus creating a balance within the two-person team. With reservation, he accepted the assignment, although, as he told me later, he was far from excited or enthusiastic about it.

This was the first time I heard about Medjugorje, a small peasant village in a very remote corner of the communist world. For almost six years, the Madonna has been visiting six children in the village, bearing messages of urgency regarding peace and love. Daily, for six years continuously . . . that's hard to believe . . . but (as I discovered later) not unbelievable!

Jim, who left skeptical, returned a different man. Jackie told me that he has prayed the rosary every day since being in Medjugorje, and now feels his life has a deeper meaning. An urgent need to communicate the message the Madonna has been giving the children burns within him now. His documentary has been well received both in and out of this country. (A copy can be purchased. See Appendix.) He still speaks of Her messages at every opportunity, lecturing several nights a week and traveling great distances to do so.

THE DECISION IS MADE . . .

Jackie's story stirred me. For some reason, after she left I couldn't stop thinking about the highly unusual events. Maybe it was due to my Catholic upbringing; but maybe not. I have previously read about the historical Marian apparitions of Lourdes and Fatima. I was amazed to hear that Marian apparitions were actually occurring now; that the mother of God was manifesting herself in our day. But I think more than that, as Jackie had continued her story, I was intrigued with the fact that the people of a small, impoverished village had undergone a complete transformation during the six-year duration of these new apparitions. Those thoughts filled me with an inner compulsion to go to Medjugorje, myself. I contacted Jackie several weeks later. She told me that not only did she want to go, but that Jim's father wanted to, as well.

The next opportunity for this sojourn just happened to be during Easter week of 1986. Traditionally, for our family, Easter is reserved for family gatherings. It was not a tradition I could breach easily. Response from some family members and friends to my new option was, basically, "I can't believe you would dump out on your family at Easter." That certainly didn't make the decision any easier for me. My immediate family, though, supported me in whichever option I chose.

After much thought and reflection, I decided that the opportunity to experience such a remarkable phenomenon during this very spiritual occasion, was one that could not be passed over lightly. Though affronted with criticism, I was compelled to make the pilgrimage. To me, such a "sacrifice" was justified in my mind, in light of the significant events Jackie had told me about. I would later realize that the sacrifice was actually a blessing in disguise.

We arranged to meet at Kennedy Airport in New York on April 11, 1987 to depart for Yugoslavia, a twenty-four hour journey. We joined approximately one hundred other people from all over the country to embark on our tour/adventure.

Such were the events preceding my visit to Medjugorje, which would indeed change my life, and lead me to write this book.

THE TRIP

I remember that Saturday afternoon in April, waiting patiently with the others at the airport for packets of information to be dispersed among us. Excited chatter was part of the continuous whirl of activity in the airport. As we became acquainted, we shared and compared information about these special events, which we hoped would soon experience for ourselves. Each person had his/her own story to tell about how he or she had heard about this little village in Yugoslavia. The stories were as different and varied as the storytellers themselves, who came from all walks of life, from everywhere in the United States. The few I spoke with personally all had one thing in common. Regardless of age or sex, there was a certain reverence, coupled with an intoxicating curiosity and determination, in spite of the forewarning that it would be a difficult and arduous journey. We were pilgrims, who thought we knew what to expect. Had the tour guides told us at that moment that the trip would be a hundred times more difficult than we expected, it would have made no difference to any of us.

We were advised that delays by communist officials were not only commonplace, but to be expected. Furthermore, the terrain of the countryside was very rocky, with many steep cliffs. There would be much climbing, unending walking, and we had been told to bring sturdy, durable walking shoes. There was no place for high heels! Mittens, scarves, hats, sweaters, and heavy coats were recommended for clothing (yes, in April!), as the weather the previous weeks had been bitter cold. Adequate heating was rare. We were told that bath facilities would be minimal, and each was to bring his own soap and towels. Later, we would see that, in fact, there was only one public restroom in the village, which was controlled by the gypsies. Correct change was required, or one was denied access. One quickly learned to be prepared, or one was out of luck! Hot water and electricity were luxuries in the village, also. We soon discovered that the briefing was far from exaggerated!

The flight to Zagreb, Yugoslavia was an eight-hour flight. Many exhibited signs of fatigue by the time we arrived. As we stepped off the plane, we were greeted by the cold blank expressions and unaccommodating attitude of the customs guards. We were delayed much longer than usual, and without apology. I was told that some tours to Medjugorje were delayed for up to two days at the airport! It seemed as if the guards tried to make life as difficult as possible. We were told, beforehand, to conduct ourselves properly, as the communist officials were seeking out intimidation and arrests. The atmosphere was somber, and smiles were lacking everywhere. A loneliness came over me as I witnessed the wholesale indifference to others. I realized as I watched, that it wasn't only the guards who were guilty of an indifferent attitude. How easy it is, even at home, in America, to isolate ourselves from each other. Amidst broken homes, suicides, alcoholism, and drug problems . . . it is there too . . . loneliness and isolation.

As weary as we were, everything seemed tedious. Things as minute as trying to buy crackers that weren't on the menu, and the presence of, much less, the lack of cooperation from, the staunch, unswerving military personnel, were not encouraging. I began to think it was as if we were part of a contest, or a game. Could we maintain our enthusiasm and excitement in such bleak surroundings, with no promise of a departure time, or even a possible departure?

I looked around observing the fabric of a very diverse, but somehow mysteriously similar group of people. We were a determined lot. There was a woman traveling alone with two babies. One of the babies was quite handicapped; the other had been, and still was, very agitated and uncomfortable. Everyone pitched in to help make the child more comfortable. The mother remained incredibly calm, with a sense of quiet perseverance about her.

There was a man in danger of losing his sight completely. He was hoping for a miracle to restore his vision. I was amazed at his positive, and hopeful attitude. I thought to myself: perhaps those of us who see and have all our physical abilities have less vision than this blinding man. As I sat, I found myself counting the many blessings I had taken for granted.

The game was no game at all. People responded with love, inspiration, and support for one another. I wondered what the guards were thinking. Was it a bit puzzling or frustrating to them, watching thousands of people come through this airport, peacefully committed to this holy experience which transcended the country and language, politics and religion? Perhaps these pilgrims they encountered every day might put them a bit more in touch with themselves, and maybe even rattle a few of them in their military boots!

Finally, after much waiting, we flew to Dubrovnik, and then boarded a bus to Medjugorje. The bus ride was very quiet as we hugged the edge of the narrow, bumpy roads intertwined through the scenic countryside. It seemed as if each of us were all in our own little worlds, trying to remember everything we'd been told, everything we'd read, and at the same time, trying to get in touch with the reality of being—really *being* in the place where the Holy Mother has been appearing to these six simple, humble children. As I watched the brilliant setting sun, I wondered if we would be witness to the miracle of the sun, written about in several books, and attested to by thousands.

We prayed the rosary, and were given a crash course in Croatian, the language of Medjugorje. We were asked to put aside all preconceived notions and be totally open to the upcoming experience, to be open to God's will and what He had to offer us. As fatigued as we were, we looked at each other and broke out in grins, grins of excitement and anticipation. We had all heard of, or read about miracles, but to be part of one? We could hardly contain our excitement!

THE AREA AND ITS HISTORY

The country of Yugoslavia is flanked by Italy, Austria, Hungary, Romania, Bulgaria, Greece, and Albania. It is approximately the size of Wyoming, with two million more people than California comprising its population of over 22 million. Yugoslavia is made up of six republics. Each possesses its own officially recognized nationality (Macedonians, Croatians, Slovenes, Serbs, Montenegrans), with the exception of Bosnia-Hercegovina. A potpourri of nationalities calls this republic home. Medjugorje is located in this republic as well. There are over fourteen languages that are recognized in Yugoslavia, and two alphabets are used, Latin and Cyrillic. There is one political party, Communist.

World War II contributed to the strife and dissention that has continuously haunted this country. Consider, that out of a total population of 15 million, 1.7 million (over 11 per cent) were killed in the battle that raged between Hitler's Nazism and Tito's Marxism. A modified form of communism emerged, wherein the state directs some sectors of the economy, and worker-chosen councils run the industries.

In 1966 Tito established diplomatic relations with the Holy See (advisory council to the Vatican). This former, predominately atheistic country is now 88 per cent religious: 50.4 per cent of Orthodox, 28.3 per cent Catholic, 8.5 per cent Moslem (a direct influence from neighboring Turkey), 0.8 per cent Protestant, and a nominal percentage are Jewish or of other faiths.

The Croatian and Slovene Catholics account for two-thirds of the entire Catholic population. Over 800,000 Croatian Catholics reside in the republic of Bosnia-Hercegovina where Medjugorje is located.

It is important to understand the troubled background of these diligent and faithful people, who were the first Slavic people to adopt Christianity. They have suffered intense periods of oppression and struggles with persecution. Within such a background, not only has there been a struggle for religious freedom, but dissention among the Catholic hierarchy, and Franciscans as well. Is it surprising that the Madonna has chosen to appear here? The location seems to have been chosen, almost as if to say, "If peace can be achieved in this microcosm of major conflict, strife, and dissention, it can be achieved anywhere."

THE ARRIVAL IN THE VILLAGE . . . THE PEOPLE . . .

By the time we actually arrived in Medjugorje, it was dusk, Sunday evening, April 12th, and we'd lost six hours. The bus pulled into the village and we were dropped off two, four, and six at a time at the home of villagers, without our luggage. We left promptly for mass. My legs and feet were very swollen. I was definitely feeling the effects of travel. Even so, mass was a special experience for me. Just being with thousands of people from all corners of the world was very moving. We then returned to our host's home for dinner around 9:00 p.m., where I became acquainted with the people I was staying with for this special journey.

In the small, previously unknown village, there are no hotels. The closest public accommodations are in Dubrovnik, about an hour and a half away. Those thousands of pilgrims who travel to Medjugorje, are hosted by the people of the town, themselves. Before the appearances of the Madonna, the village had hardly even been described as peaceful or hospitable. Even though it is peaceful now, the communist presence is never forgotten. Pilgrims are advised that any religious articles should never be visible in public, for fear of being assessed a fine (which actually occurred to an acquaintance of mine later).

I stayed at the home of Vera and Andreas and their four lovely children. I was told it was a very special privilege, as their home was one of the few that had some heaters and hot water. It was one of the finest homes in the village.

Jackie and I shared a modest room with twin beds and a small nightstand and lamp, on the top level of the house. We were indeed privileged to have a small portable heater in our room, as I would later find out. It was here that I realized how many things we, in the United States, take for granted: things as simple as choosing and visiting a doctor to making a phone call. In Medjugorje, the people in the village must travel great distances for medical care. Our phone books list pages of physicians, in close proximity, from which we can choose. We simply call for appointments, as we do for a myriad of needs throughout the day. It can take up to four days by telephone to reach someone in the United States from Medjugorje!

The attitude of the villagers who hosted our tour group was

unbelievable to people from a country where you lock bedroom windows, car doors, and gates every night. The communists take approximately 60 per cent of the tour money which goes to the village. A small portion of the remaining money is given to the host families to cover the cost of bed and board. In fact, what is left is hardly enough to cover the cost of the food! Furthermore, there is no seeming respite from the influx of tourists. As soon as our bus left on Saturday, another arrived the same day. At one point, I asked our hostess, via our interpreter, Dragon, "Do you ever experience fatigue, or do you ever want to hang out a sign that says, 'Gone on Vacation?' " She laughed softly and said, ". . . as we send out love, it can only come back to us."

Such were the words that came from the same woman who not only had her own family of six to care for, but ten additional household guests, as well! She was an inspiration to me, and would become a friend as well. In our group, there was a Catholic nun, two Catholic priests (one from Ireland), a gentleman from New York, the tour guide and his wife, a friend of theirs, James, Jackie, and myself. In addition, each night there were extra visitors, some still arriving at 11:00 p.m. Vera was up at the crack of dawn and was always gracious, no matter what time of day . . . or night. She welcomed each and every guest with her warm smile and open, loving heart. Vera prepared at least sixteen hot meals, three times daily, at six seatings. Her own family ate separately from us. Then there was the washing and the cleaning which had been going on for six years! It certainly was not for financial reward that this woman worked so unselflessly. There was little question in my mind that this woman, speaking so unassumingly, was surely speaking from her heart. The people I encountered and experienced in Medjugorje seemed to have found something very special in their lives, and demonstrated it consistently in their behavior, deeds, and through their inspiring examples.

In spite of the long day, we stayed up late that first evening, visiting, in excitement and anticipation of the coming events. Everyone finally went to sleep, and 8:30 a.m. came early. After breakfast we were off to mass. There were prayer and healing services, and a basic tour of the village.

We walked everywhere. The walking, which was at first tedious, became a joy. I became more aware of the change in temperatures, the beautiful sky, the trees, the abundant fields over-flowing with blossoming broccoli, grape arbors, and other harvests. I saw families all working together in the fields. As I paused for a moment to watch these families working together joyfully, my mind wondered. I recalled my husband, Tommy, summoning the family to such a simple task as the annual leaf raking, and the groans which followed.

I also witnessed with admiration the reverence and respect shown to the aging matriarchs of the area. The youngest children were playing ball in the paths through the fields and narrow streets of the village. It was a slice of simple life. I had to travel thousands of miles to see it. It was as if the Madonna, the universal matriarch, was saying to each of us: live simple lives in joy and peace, find the glory in little things.

That night, the priest from Ireland, who was also staying in the same home, was allowed into the room of apparitions, the small room in the rectory of St. James Church where the daily apparitions appear to the children. As we gathered for dinner, he shared his experience of awe and wonder as he witnessed the two visionaries praying the rosary. What was most impressive to him was the great degree of reverence these young people exhibited.

We all looked forward to the events to come.

CLIMBING KRIZEVAK . . . THE ROOM OF APPARITIONS

The third day of our visit brought some of the most moving personal experiences of the journey. It was on this day that we embarked on a grueling climb up the holy mountain, Mt. Krizevak. Afterwards, we joined the crowd of people outside the church hoping for an opportunity to enter the room of apparitions.

The day began early with mass, followed by the ascension up the steep and rocky mountain. As we climbed, we could see the many crosses marking each station of the cross. Most pilgrims anticipated the trek across sacred ground, in hopes of experiencing their own miracle, or personal confirmation of the apparitions. Many had left personal belongings and offerings, strewn on the crosses along the path up the mountain. They came, leaving behind not only their gifts, but offerings from others unable to make the pilgrimage themselves, in hopes of some personal miracle, blessing, or healing. The twelve stations of the cross were said as we climbed. At each station, we stopped to pray and reflect on the crucifixion and the significance of the Easter season. Four hours later, after a weary and tiring climb, we found ourselves at the bottom of the mountain again.

Upon returning to the village around 4:00 p.m., we joined the throngs of people waiting outside the church of St. James. To my amazement, people from all over the world converged outside the walls of the rectory, waiting and hoping to be one of the twenty selected to enter the room of apparitions. The selection process was determined in this order: handicapped, clergy, special guests, with special needs, and randomly selected individuals from the crowd gathered outside. After an hour and a half of waiting in the freezing cold, I was ecstatic to be chosen as one of the select few. At 5:30, we entered the room of apparitions. Once a priest's bedroom, this small, sparse room was furnished with a bookcase, cot, and a small wooden bench. As on the crosses at Krizevak, the room was laden with personal artifacts. The room was more than filled with the twenty anxious and expectant visitors. Clenched in my hand was the white-beaded rosary with its thin silver chain that Jim Bailey had given me for Christmas—the key which had prophetically lead me to this tiny crowded room. I waited in anticipation for the visionaries and the prayer to begin. I was visibly moved when the two visionaries, Marija and Jakov, arrived quietly and unobtrusively. They knelt at the door. Marija smiled at and touched a small child. About 5:34, the seers led us in praying the rosary with them. In front of me, I recognized the face of a child who had been on the plane from New York with me. She was saying her prayers so reverently. I was moved, and continued to pray, myself. After these prayers, the visionaries moved to the center of the room, before the cross. They walked ever so carefully, so as not to disturb, or step on anyone. They were now almost directly in front of me. The seers spontaneously dropped to their knees in synchronicity. I saw them bless themselves. The actual apparition lasted only a brief time— maybe less than two minutes. During this time, I noticed that my rosary beads were illuminated with little pink lights. I looked around to see others glowing also. Was this a blessing? We closed, singing "Ave Ave." I was overcome with emotion. I could hear hundreds of voices outside singing with us. They were people who had been waiting patiently for hours. I was so fortunate! Indescribable emotions filled me. This soul-stirring experience was something that I will never forget.

THE CHURCH . . . THE STATE OF THE PARISH

A terrible religious conflict began in Yugoslavia during World War II between the Catholic Croats and the Orthodox Serbs. The Croatian government of this newly-created communist state pledged its allegiance to the Roman Catholic Church. Desiring Catholicism to flourish, and apparently following Hitler's example, this government then embarked on a bloody attempt to persecute and eliminate all Orthodox Serbs. Still, today, these atrocities of the past have not been forgiven. The Serbian Orthodox bishops have remained very persistent in their insistence that the Pope demand an apology from the Croatian Catholic bishops for past events. Although the Croatian bishops would like to reconcile their differences, they feel an apology would implicate the Catholic Church for the persecutions, rather than the political regime at the time.

In addition, Franciscan bishops have governed the Mostar diocese (where Medjugorje is located) for centuries. In 1942, a diocesan priest was appointed Bishop of Mostar. The new bishop requested the transfer of several Franciscan parishes to his diocesan clergy. In 1967, and again in 1975, the Holy See (advisory council to the Vatican) ordered the transfer of several Franciscan parishes. However, after forty years of strife, and two mandates, these seven parishes still remain Franciscan.

It was in the midst of not only political and cultural dissention, but religious chasm, as well, that the Holy Mother first appeared in this troubled, remote village in June, 1981.

Before the apparitions, the parish could be described as a typical parish, very similar to many in the United States. Prayer was waning, commitment was faltering, and as Father Tomislav Vlasic said, the villagers were churchgoers "more than in other regions of Yugoslavia, but they were already on the road of a declining faith." (*The Queen of Peace Visits Medjugorje*, page 12.)

The state of the parish, and how it has been affected by the apparitions is best explained by Father Tomislav Vlasic, former parish priest, who delivered the following in a sermon to Italian pilgrims on August 15, 1983:

Before the apparitions, the people of the parish . . . were annoyed when Mass lasted more than 45 minutes. After the apparitions, they remained in church for three hours or more and after returning home prayed some more. They prayed in the fields, in their cars— everywhere. On the average, all families pray one hour a day.

The churches everywhere are always full of people and especially young people.

The people here fast every Friday on bread and water. Many people and many families fast twice a week. There are some who make a total fast, eating and drinking nothing all day. The only food they take is the Eucharist, yet they work, sometimes at hard labor.

The young people lead the way. They pray and fast more than others.

The people who live here do not ask themselves whether or not the apparitions are true. They say: "We no longer believe, we know. We now have a new life. We do not want to retrograde. We do not want our previous life with its pains and litigations. Now we are happy and we definitely want to continue this way." (*The Queen of Peace Visits Medjugorje*, pages 86-87.)

In *Queen of Peace, Echo Of The Eternal Word*, (page 27.), Father Tomislav Pervan writes,

The message proclaimed through the apparitions of the Mother of God has had a tremendous impact on the lives of the visionaries, the parish and the people generally. People were reached in the totality of life); first they were frightened, then came renewal, change and the reversal of life styles.

It is obvious that the coming of the apparitions at Medjugorje has had a profound effect on the people who live near them.

Chapter 2

In the Beginning

"One can't believe impossible things . . . " [said Alice] "I dare say you haven't had much practice," said the Queen. "When I was your age I always did it for up to half-an-hour a day. Why sometimes I've believed as many as six impossible things before breakfast."

ALICE THROUGH THE LOOKING GLASS
—Lewis Carroll

SEQUENCE OF EVENTS

Crisis is God's design to help us out and accomplish solidarity—a coming together in love." Crisis might well be the word to describe what these six children were confronted with when the apparitions began. What occurred on the first day, June 24, 1981, would issue forth a turmoil that would catapult the lives of the children, and indeed the community, into a new understanding of a faith they had previously taken for granted.

That Wednesday in June was the feast of John the Baptist, who interestingly enough, in the New Testament, is proclaimed as the forerunner of Jesus Christ. (Personally, as I became more intrigued with the events at Medjugorje, I could not help but be interested in the connection of Mary appearing to warn the world on the feast day of the one who was chosen to announce, as it were, the coming of Christ.)

THE FIRST DAY: Wednesday, June 24, 1981

It was late afternoon when Ivanka Ivankovic and Mirjana Dragicevic, whose families live near Medjugorje (in Bijakovici), were walking through a sheep pasture near Mt. Podbrdo. It was Ivanka who

25

first noticed a luminous silhouette in front of her. She appeared to be a young Croatian woman, with blue eyes, black hair, pink cheeks, and a long silver robe with a white veil. It was as if she was suspended in mid-air on a little grey cloud, a few hundred years away. Her face shone gently on them. The surprised and uncertain Ivanka exclaimed, "Mirjana, look there is Gospa—Our Lady." (*The Queen of Peace Visits Medjugorje*, page 13.) Unconcerned, and not even bothering to look, Mirjana said, "Come on! Would our Lady appear to us?" (*The Queen of Peace Visits Medjugorje*, page 13.)

The two girls, perplexed and confused, hurriedly left the field to find their friends. At this point, the reference materials vary in their accounts of the event. Consistent in all the accounts is the following information. The two girls shared their incredible story with at least one other friend, who, of course, passed the fascinating story on. Ivanka and Mirjana then returned to the site of Ivanka's vision, either by themselves or with one friend, thirteen-year old Milka Pavlovic. Again the apparition appeared. While the vision remained, all references agreed that three other youths, Vicka Ivankovic (seventeen), Ivan Ivankovic (twenty), and Ivan Dragicevic (sixteen), were also present and witnessed the apparition. The six astonished youths all recognized the Madonna, but were too overwhelmed to speak to her. Ivanka later described "Our Lady" holding the Christ Child, as if to show them that She was indeed the Holy Mother. As the young people watched in wonder, the Holy Mother called them to come up the mountain to Her. Although too afraid to move, the children strangely felt at peace, and remained until the vision ended about forty-five minutes after it first appeared.

Upon their arrival in the village, they told people what they had seen, though none believed them. Milka's sister, Marija, laughed at her, while Vicka's sister told her, with somber sarcasm, that she had seen a flying saucer. Nevertheless, such an event caused much curious chattering, which continued into the night. As each villager went to sleep that night, they wondered what had really happened, and what might happen in the morning. No one wondered more than the children themselves.

DAY 2: Thursday, June 25, 1981

Three of the children, Ivanka, Mirjana, and Vicka could not contain their curiosity. They decided to return to Mt. Podbrdo that next evening, after their day's work in the tobacco fields. They returned about the same time the vision occurred the day before. Two of the youths that were present on the first day did not return, and have not seen the Madonna since. Ivan Ivankovic felt the escapade was childish. Milka Pavlovic had to remain at home and work, although her mother allowed her skeptical sister, Marija, to go. (Marija, the previous day, thought her sister was hallucinating.) The three original girls, Ivanka Ivankovic (fifteen), Mirjana Dragicevic (sixteen), and Vicka Ivankovic (seventeen) were accompanied by two adults, presumably as witnesses. A few other youths, including Ivan Dragicevic (sixteen), Marija Pavlovic (sixteen) and Jakov Colo (ten), also tagged along.

It was this group of six children, ranging in age from ten to seventeen, who would constitute the core group of visionaries.

Again, Ivanka first sighted the Madonna, who, from high above them on Mt. Podbrdo, beckoned them to come to Her. Vicka recounted the amazing events that followed:

> We ran quickly up the hill. It was not like walking on the ground. Nor did we look for the path. We simply ran toward Her. In five minutes we were up the hill, as if something had pulled us through the air. I was afraid. I was also barefoot, yet no thorns had scratched me. (*The Queen of Peace Visits Medjugorje*, page 15.)

Within five minutes, only these select children had covered ground that normally takes twenty minutes when walking at a very brisk pace! Those accompanying them were unable to follow and fell behind. Once at the top, compelled by an unknown force, the children were virtually thrown to their knees.

> When we were about two meters (six feet) away from the Madonna, we felt as if we were thrown to our knees. Jakov was thrown kneeling into a thorny bush and I thought he would be injured. But he came out of it without a scratch. (*The Queen of Peace Visits Medjugorje*, page 15.)

Ivanka was the first to actually address the Madonna, asking about her mother who had died unexpectedly only the month before. Although Ivanka's mother had been a good woman and mother, she had not been a devout Catholic. Our Lady said she was well and with Her and that she shouldn't worry about her. Later, the villagers would be encouraged by this response, as they realized that one did not have to perform extraordinary acts to enter "the kingdom of Heaven." This exchange, and the response of the villagers to it, is significant in light of the true universality of the apparitions, and their messages. Indeed, it would appear that the Madonna has come for all children, for Catholics, and for non-Catholics, as well with Her simple messages of peace and love.

Mirjana also addressed the Madonna on that second day, after Ivanka. What she asked indicated the individual concerns of the children, not only to the extraordinary events that were taking place, but also to the reactions of the disbelieving villagers. She recounted the reactions from the previous day, when the response was that the children were "crazy." Although the Madonna responded with a smile, there was no promise for any sign to confirm the visionaries' experiences to the world.

It is interesting to note that during this apparition, Vicka asked Mirjana what time it was. While looking at her watch, Mirjana observed that the number twelve was no longer a twelve, but a nine. The children felt this was a miracle. It seemed that the Madonna gave the children this sign, to confirm the apparitions, and Her presence to them. To this day, it is said that Mirjana still has this "unique" watch.

The subtle signs which would follow would, themselves, be an integral part of the transforming experience in faith and understanding, not only for the children and the villagers, but for the world as well.

The apparitions continued to occur everyday, and have been occurring until this time. The earliest apparitions seem to have been concerned primarily with orienting the children, and the community; in essence, preparing them for the messages to come. Most of the apparitions are concerned with messages of prayer and will be addressed specifically in chapter 5.

DAY 3: Friday, June 26, 1981

By the third day, June 26, news of the visions had spread, and a crowd of several thousand circled the visionaries at the base of Mt. Podbrdo. For the first time, the Madonna's apparition was preceded by a brilliant light that was witnessed not only by the children, but the spectators as well. The light illuminated not only the area, but the entire village!

The overwhelming crowd and stifling heat were more than some of the children could bear, and Ivanka, Mirjana, and Vicka fainted. They were revived, and the apparition that followed lasted approximately thirty minutes. When Ivanka asked the Madonna why She was appearing, She responded, "I have come because there are many believers here. I want to be with you to convert and reconcile everyone." (*The Queen of Peace Visits Medjugorje*, page 20.) The children then asked Her if She would come again and She indicated She would and closed with the closing that She would continue to emphasize in these initial visits, "Go in the peace of God."

DAY 4: Saturday, June 27, 1981

By Saturday morning, the police were watching the children. It was also on this day that the parish priest was made aware of tape recorded documentation of the events, which would later be confiscated.

The children were summoned to police headquarters in Citluk that afternoon, and in spite of persistent inquiries, none denied the apparitions. Later, the children were sent to a doctor to ascertain their physical and mental health. After short examinations, the youths were released with a clean bill of health.

The authorities were not the only ones concerned with the events. Adults in the religious community were wondering about the veracity of the purported experiences, and decided to submit the children to a test to establish whether or not the apparitions were actually occurring. A few villagers decided to divide the visionaries into two groups, wondering whether the apparitions would still occur and hoping that the children would have conflicting stories, if indeed, they saw the Madonna. This would certainly put an end to the entire affair! However, the events that followed could not have been further from their expectations!

One group was sent to the top of the mountain, while the other remained at the base of the mountain, both of course, being sites of previous apparitions. At the bottom of the mountain were only Marija and Jakov (Ivan had not joined the other five), with two adults at their sides. For a second time the apparition was preceded by a light. This time, though, it was witnessed by the children alone. The Madonna beckoned the children to Her side, and Marija proceeded to run at such a tremendous speed, that the two adults (one being the priest from the church) were unable to keep up with her. Later Marija described the feeling as that of being led effortlessly to the top. While the others, including Jakov, reached the top, the very perplexed Marija stated that the Madonna had disappeared. Now the children, all together again at the top of the mountain, dropped to their knees. Preceding the next apparition, and witnessed by the throngs gathered around the children, was a brilliant, undeniable light.

Ivanka asked the figure who She was. The response was, "I am the Blessed Virgin Mary." (*The Queen of Peace Visits Medjugorje*, page 25.) This is important to note, because it is the first time the Madonna actually identified Herself to the children.

Vicka asked Her to prove to the people who were present that She, was indeed, there. Her reply was that those who could not see Her should believe as though they were seeing. This was strikingly similar to Christ's apparitions after the Crucifixion, wherein He confronts a doubting Thomas. "You believe because you can see me. Happy are those who have not seen and yet believe." (John 20:27; 29) The Madonna then disappeared.

The children remained on the mountain, thinking perhaps the Holy Mother would appear, as She had not parted with Her "customary" farewell of peace. After waiting a long time, they left, only to stop halfway down the mountain to be greeted by Her once again. At this point, She addressed them as Her "dear angels," and indicated that She would return again the next day at the same time and place, and departed saying, "Go in the peace of God."

The Madonna also appeared to Ivan, even though he did not accompany the group to Mt. Podbrdo. His parents asked him not to, as they were concerned for his well-being in light of the increased attention and publicity concerning the apparitions. The Holy Mother appeared to him as he was walking a short distance from the village, and told him to have courage, and most importantly, to be at peace.

If the members of the parish had doubts previously, they were quickly being dissipated. The children were separated, and the apparitions still occurred, not once, but several times. Furthermore, Ivan, apart and alone, witnessed the Madonna as well.

DAY 5: Sunday, June 28, 1981

By the fifth day, interest had heightened, and the crowd had increased to an amazing fifteen thousand. The visionaries returned to Mt. Podbrdo at 6:30 p.m., the time designated by the Madonna. At exactly 6:30, the Holy Mother appeared, and the children asked prepared questions. These questions, with their responses, were recorded by a nearby observer.

When asked why the apparitions were not seen in the church by everyone, the Madonna repeated Her previous response, "Blessed are they who have not seen and who believe." The children then asked, "What do You want of these people gathered here?" Our Lady gazed at the multitudes and smiled, saying, "That they believe without seeing." (all these quotes, *The Queen of Peace Visits Medjugorje*, page 29.) Then the Madonna disappeared. The children, now expecting the familiar departing words, "Go in the peace of God," again waited for another appearance, and began praying. Once again, She appeared, reiterating upon the children's repeated questioning, that She wanted those to believe who did not see. She ended with the anticipated "Go in the peace of God," and in Her place, was a light, which only the children witnessed.

By now it seemed clear that the apparitions would only be seen by the children, and an important attendant aspect of the appearances would be that the thousands of visitors would endure a test of faith. This would become a part of the experience of pilgrims coming to Medjugorje. The test of faith was "believing without seeing," knowing that the Truth always begins within.

DAY 6: Monday, June 29, 1981

On Monday, June 29, interest in the children was building, and they were summoned, once again, to Citluk for additional questioning. This time, the intent was to discredit their psychological stability. Once again, the children were examined by yet another doctor, and found to be of sound mind and body. Again, they were released.

The youths went home, and returned to the mountain that evening. They began praying and Our Lady appeared. The children, under heavy pressure from the villagers and local authorities, pleaded with the Madonna for a miracle, for proof, so that all would believe them.

It was on this sixth day that the children also requested the first of many healings on a small mute boy named Daniel. The detailed events of this healing are described in chapter 4, Signs and Wonders. The Madonna's response was consistent with the message she had been emphasizing for the last few days, "Let them (Daniel's parents) believe firmly that he will be healed." (*The Queen of Peace Visits Medjugorje*, page 32.) He was. It is interesting that such a sign was delivered during a very critical and vulnerable period for the children, who were already being persecuted and taunted. There was doubt not only among the government authorities, but the clergy of the Parish as well, who, up to this point, had cautiously refrained from any direct involvement.

Afterwards, as on the previous day, the children discussed the day's apparitions with select villagers. The conversation was again taped.

DAY 7: Tuesday, June 20, 1981

If any day could be said to have been a landmark in supporting the truth of the children's story, it was this day. Government officials, wanting to end the apparitions and the increased publicity, decided to deter the children from their evening visit to Mt. Podbrdo. The apparitions would cease, and the entire affair would be ended. They sent two female "social workers" from Bijakovici to collect the children. Ivan was not present. The youths were told to get in the car, to see if the apparitions would occur elsewhere.

The visionaries were hurriedly taken on a tour, ending up in Cerno at the time the apparitions had been taking place. As the trip continued, the children insisted that the driver stop the car. After persistent requests, the driver acquiesced, and the children stepped out and began praying. In the sight of Mt. Podbrdo, and in unison, the youths looked up at the mountain where thousands of people were gathered. They saw a brilliant light, which began to move toward them. Ivanka then asked the women if they could see the light as well. Stunned, the social workers said that they could. Once again, the Madonna appeared.

Concerned at having digressed from the previous days' routine of meeting on Mt. Podbrdo, Mirjana asked the Holy Mother if she minded that they had accompanied the social workers. The Madonna replied no. The children then asked if the apparitions could be moved from the mountain to the church, and were told that they could. Silence followed, as the Madonna watched the children for a long time. Finally, She slowly left, saying, "Go in the peace of God." In Her wake once again was the light.

This was the first day the apparitions appeared at a site other than the vicinity of Mt. Podbrdo. It will become known that the site was not significant. In the future, the apparitions would be seen in many locations.

When the children returned to the village, they reported to Father Jozo, the parish priest. He recorded their conversation. They related that the apparitions would probably be occurring at the church in the future. The children were then informed that one of their close friends had been taken to the police for questioning. Pained and concerned, in spite of the time and the trying events of the day, the children went to the station to assure the police that their friend was in no way related to the apparitions.

A very exhausted group of children went to sleep that night, and the following days would offer no respite from the events that had materially changed their lives. There would be no going back now. The children, though they would be subjected to rigorous and sometimes ridiculous testing, would never swerve from their devotion, loyalty, and connection with the Holy Mother. It would be a relationship that not only altered their lives, but would change the lives of millions of others who would come in hope of witnessing the Light of the Madonna at Medjugorje.

DAY 8: Wednesday, July 1, 1981

Until this time, the church's attitude had remained quiet and conservative. Although the pastor, Father Jozo, had been in continual contact with the visionaries, he did not himself believe in their authenticity. His role had been that of advisor and counselor . . . a minister, as it were. This position would change dramatically today, and the priest would not only become an avid supporter of the children, but he himself would soon be witness to an apparition. This would support him in his role as leader of the faithful and religious community.

To date, the government has been unsuccessful in halting the apparitions. The episode with the social workers had not only failed, but the women, themselves, had handed in their resignations, attesting to the intensity and validity of the experiences. By now the police had decided to intervene directly, and try to prevent the seers from going to the site that had been the cause of such a stir. Hearing of this, the children fled the site, on foot. They were pursued by the police across the countryside towards the church.

Father Jozo was praying in the church. What followed was something he would never forget. "Something happened that for me was important and decisive . . . a turning point and a moment of revelation. While I was praying, I heard a voice say, 'Come out and protect the children.' " (*The Queen of Peace Visits Medjugorje*, page 39.) He went outside, to see the children running up the hill, crying out that the police were chasing them. Quickly, he hid them in an unoccupied room in the church and locked them in.

The police arrived shortly thereafter, and asked if the priest had seen the children. Father Jozo pointed towards the town of Bijakovici, and the police left in hot pursuit. He then returned to the unoccupied room. Concerned for their safety, he kept the children there.

Later, Father Jozo recalled a local law that disallowed questioning a minor without the permission of his parents. The parents, informed of this law, denied permission. The police were forced to abandon their questioning temporarily.

The first apparition to occur in the church happened that same day. It would not be until later that summer that Father Jozo would, himself, witness a silent apparition. This affirmation of the truth would guide him to lead the parish towards accepting the messages of the Madonna—that they might become believers without seeing—a truly faithful community.

After several incidences and a frightening chase by the police, it would seem that if the children were participating in some sort of prank, the activity would cease. To the contrary, not only did they remain true to their story, but they revealed that yet another apparition had occurred that same day. If the children were lying, they certainly would not have continued to affirm their experience, much less claim another visitation. Rather after such a harrowing chase, one would think they would have learned their lesson, and abandoned the tale. Still, they persisted in revealing messages from personal apparitions, as the apparitions continued, in the unoccupied room for the next seven days.

SIGNIFICANT EVENTS CONTINUE TO UNFOLD . . .

Sometime between July 9th and August 12th, the youths met in the church and prayed, but the Madonna did not appear. This continued for five days. When the visits resumed, the youths asked the Madonna why She had not appeared those five days to them. The Holy Mother responded that it was, indeed, a test of their faith. She wanted to know whether they would continue to meet in prayer, even if She didn't appear. Would they, too, believe without seeing?

AUGUST, 1981: IN THE THICK OF THE SUMMER HEAT

On August 7th, the Holy Mother summoned the six children to Mt. Podbrdo at two in the morning, a very peculiar time! She related an unusual message. During this vision, the Madonna promised, for the first time, a special sign, an affirmation of Her presence so others would believe also. Unfortunately, this was not to be an immediate sign.

By the 12th of August, the police were again attempting to interfere and halt the apparitions. They issued a decree placing the site of apparitions on Mt. Podbrdo off limits to the public. The apparitions never occurred here again, but continued in homes, on the hills, and in private places. Because of the increasing danger of retribution from the local authorities, secrecy was required when apparitions occurred in private residences, so as not to endanger those involved. The apparitions usually occurred when the children were together, and the focus of the messages revolved around singing and praying. The focus of the public messages that would follow in the next six years was on prayer. It is almost as if the Madonna was teaching the children to pray; that they might understand the importance of prayer, and convey that to their fascinated, attentive audiences.

By the middle of August, heat and pressure were not only on the children, and the thousands who were now believers, but on Father Jozo, as well. On August 17th, the police raided the church, locked the nuns in one of the rooms in the church and arrested the pastor, Father Jozo. The church records, which included the most accurate documentation of the events to date, were all confiscated. This is the reason much of the information available on these days is sketchy. The documentation is still being withheld.

At the end of August, Ivan, who had been conspicuously absent, went to a seminary in Dubrovnik. Remember, Ivan's mother had requested that he not accompany the group on the fourth day, and he was not present during several subsequent apparitions. Although there have been times when the children were unable to gather together, the Madonna has continued to appear to them individually, wherever they might be, as long as they are in prayer. When Ivan entered the seminary, he was privy again, to a private apparition, wherein the Madonna indicated that Her visits would cease until he had become adjusted to his new way of life. Ivan did not see Her again for seven days. Upon reappearing, the Madonna agreed to visit Ivan at two in the afternoon, rather than the usual evening time, to accommodate his new schedule and routine at the seminary.

SEPTEMBER, 1981

On September 4th, the Madonna shared more information about "the sign" with the visionaries. This sign will become one of the ten identical secrets shared with each of the six seers. The ten secrets and their significance will be discussed later. The Holy Mother said that "the sign" would be forthcoming when the apparitions ceased. Later that month, She revealed the precise date of "the sign" to five of the seers. They were not to reveal this date until permission was given.

OCTOBER, 1981

Father Jozo was tried and convicted of disobedience and encouraging unrest in the community on October 21st and 22nd. He was sentenced to three and a half years in prison. During the two days of his trial and conviction, many signs and wonders were witnessed by the villagers on Mt. Krizevak. The concrete cross on the mountain became a column of light and a silhouette of a woman (the Madonna) was seen on the hill.

The people of the town mounted a small uprising protesting the harsh sentence. The government eventually relented . . . eighteen months later. A changed Father Jozo would return to Medjugorje.

1982: THE APPARITIONS CONTINUE

By the beginning of 1982, the Madonna was consistently appearing in a small room in the Church of St. James. This general pattern has remained for the past four years, although the children receive private visitations as well, outside the church.

Several significant events occurred in this year that followed the first months of the apparitions that would lend themselves to the stability and validity of the children's story. These events would create a greater foundation for acceptance and support from the parishioners and villagers.

In August, Father Tomislav Pervan, a friend and confidante of Marijana's, was appointed third pastor to Medjugorje. Father Jozo, remember, was in prison. Father Zrinko, who replaced him, resigned under the rigor and pressure of a changing community. It is Father Pervan who still remains the pastor of St. James.

It was during this year that the Holy Mother told the children that She would reveal to each of them separately, ten sequential secrets. Each of the children would receive the secrets at different times, and was not to reveal them to anyone, under any circumstances, until instructed to do so.

By December of 1982, Mirjana became the first to receive all ten secrets. On December 25th, she received the last secret. The Madonna told her that She would only appear in the future to Mirjana on her birthday, March 18th, and in times of need. Apparently, due to the significance and importance of the secrets, she has received apparitions since then, as the content of the secrets is evidently a heavy burden for the young girl to bear. The Holy Mother, then, comes in times of need, as a loving mother, to support and sustain faith in her children. To date, the other children, with the exception of Ivanka, still have not received all ten secrets. The secrets will be discussed further in chapter 4, Signs and Wonders.

Finally, a most significant event occurred in December. It was on December 15, 1982, that Jelena Vasilj, a ten-year-old girl, began receiving messages from the Madonna by inner locution—that is to say that she began hearing the messages in her heart. It has been described by Saint Theresa of Avila as the "eyes of the soul." Although she does not receive the secrets, the Madonna has told Jelena that her path is one of a spiritual nature, to be focused in prayer.

As with the visionaries, Jelena's visitations are preceded by prayer. One other child, Marijana Vasilj (no relation to Jelena), would also receive messages from the Holy Mother via inner locutions, but her visitations did not begin until 1983.

1983: STILL MORE TO COME

After eighteen months in prison, a very humble Father Jozo was released on February 17th. He returned to Medjugorje. Shortly thereafter, he left the village. About his painful, but very spiritual experience, he said, "Every good priest should see the inside of a jail and suffer for the faith. I discovered in prison what the Catholic faith is and the strength and dignity of a life being offered." (*The Queen of Peace Visits Medjugorje*, page 49.)

March 19, 1983 brought another young girl, Marijana Vasilj, into this widening picture. Being a close friend of Jelena's, Marijana was visiting on that day. In Jelena's home, Marijana saw a white cloud which transformed into the Madonna. She, too, would receive "inner" messages, inner locutions, in the days, months, and years which followed.

In the spring of 1983, the Madonna told the world, through the children, "Hasten your conversion. Do not wait for the sign that has been announced. For the non-believers it will be too late for them to have a conversion. You who believe, be converted and deepen your faith."

In late May, the Madonna asked eleven-year-old Jelena to inform the priest that a parish prayer group should be formed. The priest designated Tuesday nights as the evening this group of young people (average age of twenty) would gather for spiritual guidance via instructions and prayer. The Madonna said that She would lead the group and guide it in holiness of life, through Jelena. Until his departure from Medjugorje in 1984, Father Tomislav Vlasic related the guidance and instruction Jelena received from the Holy Mother. Marija Pavlovic, the only one of the six visionaries who is a member of this group, also relates the teachings. The conditions of membership follow:

> To begin with, they have to renounce everything and put themselves entirely in God's hands. They must renounce all fear; abandonment to God has no place for fear. All the difficulties that they meet will work for their spiritual growth and for the glory of God . . . . I prefer young people because married people have family and work obligations. But everyone who wants to take part in this program can do so . . . . (*Medjugorje Unfolds, Mary Speaks to the World*, page 41.)

A commitment to the group of at least four years was required. No member was to make any other commitment, to marriage or even romantic attachments, profession, or religious life during this time. About sixty young people and four older women responded to this new call. A one-month period was established by the Madonna to allow each member ample time to reassess his/her commitment, and change his/her mind, if they so chose.

The first meeting of this group dealt with loving their enemies, blessing, and praying for them. The Madonna said, "I know that you are not able to love your enemies, but I beg you to pray every day at least five minutes to the Sacred Heart and to my Heart and we will give you divine love with which you will be able to love even your enemies." (*The Queen of Peace Visits Medjugorje*, page 99.)

The second meeting involved a reprimand. The Holy Mother kindly said, "You have begun to pray three hours a day and this is good. But, you keep looking at your watches and worrying about the numerous things you will have to do after the meeting. If you continue doing this, you will not be able to fulfill these duties properly, nor will you be able to advance spiritually. You must renounce your preoccupations and be ready so that the Spirit can lead and guide you interiorly. Only in this way, can you advance spiritually. When you do this, you will discover that you have the time to complete all your duties and also have time left over." (*The Queen of Peace Visits Medjugorje*, page 99.)

Responding to continued calls to personal holiness through prayer, Jelena's prayer group was now meeting Thursday and Saturday evenings, as well as Tuesday nights. The group consistently met at 9:00 p.m. after the evening mass. The meetings usually lasted about two hours. During that year, the Madonna also suggested that members of this group meet, in pairs, at other times to share heartfelt thoughts of God, faith, difficulties, and/or problems. After a while, though, She recommended that at these times, only faith, prayer and peace were to be discussed, in lieu of other topics. "That kind of sharing, She said, is also prayer." (*Medjugorje Unfolds, Mary Speaks to the World,* page 42.) The members of this group have developed their ability to love anyone they come in contact with, including disbelievers and opponents of their faith. They have learned to harbor no anger or resentment in their lives. They also ask God, daily, to bless the world and all its inhabitants. The group members contended that what appeared to be sacrifices to others. *i.e.*, the original commitments made to the Madonna were truly blessings which have enriched their lives beyond our comprehension.

The Thursday night meetings of this prayer group seemed to focus on public messages, for the parish, and all people of the world. Beginning on March 1, 1984, these weekly public messages, usually spoken through Marija, were recorded. Transcripts of these weekly Marian messages are available (See Appendix.)

By the summer of 1984, the apparitions which had lasted as long as forty-five minutes, were now lasting only a minute, sometimes less. At the end of May, in an apparition to Ivan, Our Lady requested that in preparation of Her birthday, on August 5th, the villagers begin a three-day fast and remain in prayer. Once again, at the end of July, She appeared to Ivan, stressing the importance of the silent actions of prayer and fasting. She emphasized that these actions reflected the state of the heart and soul more than words, and that those participating by virtue of the activity of the soul, would be cared for. She seemed to indicate that *all* willing people, whether physically in her presence in Medjugorje, or spiritually present, in the privacy of their hearts, could be part of the transforming experience.

The response was overwhelming, not only in Medjugorje, but in the United States as well, where hundreds of people participated in the requested fasting and prayer.

By August 5th, there were an estimated 35,000 people gathered for the celebration honoring the 2,000th birthday of the Holy Mother. It was on this day, early in the morning, for the first recorded time, that many would personally witness a vision of the Madonna on Mt. Krizevak. There were thousands who had camped outside the church, itself. They saw what has been described as the silhouette of a woman clothed in brilliant white, her hands raised towards the sky. Some reported seeing the figure in colored garments. All who were witnesses said it was something that could never be forgotten, that they would always have it etched in their memories, a vision unlike anything they had ever seen on earth. Many others reported other signs and wonders that day, including the sun spinning furiously in its orbit.

Since then, these signs and wonders occur in a three to four-week frequency, lasting for up to four days at a time. (Details of specific signs and wonders will be discussed in chapter 4.)

It is very interesting that the apparitions, which maintained some consistency as far as the children are concerned, were also witnessed by many others. There is no pattern to the others who have witnessed the vision, nor is there any explanation. It seems that the witnessing of the Holy Mother by so many different and diverse groups lends support to the children and their visions. Of course, each person who has been witness has experienced personal revelations and growth that will touch and change them in ways the world will never know.

1985: IVANKA RECEIVES THE LAST SECRET

April 2, 1985 brought another change in location of the apparitions. On that date, the Madonna began appearing to the visionaries in a small room in the rectory of St. James Church. The apparitions continued to occur there, until the site would again be changed in late 1987.

On May 6, 1985, Ivanka received the last secret. Jakov, Ivan, and Marija were gathered in the rectory with Ivanka, and had finished receiving their messages. They looked over and noticed Ivanka was still in an altered state, listening to the Madonna. She was told the final secret, and instructed not to return to the rectory the following day, but to wait at home for another visit.

The following is an intimate, and touching account of one of this young girl's final apparitions, wherein she was allowed to see her natural mother. She had questioned the Madonna about her deceased mother in the first year of apparitions. Ivanka told Father Slvako Barbaric the following:

> As on every other day, Our Lady came with the greeting, "Praised be Jesus." I responded, "May Jesus and Mary always be praised."
>
> I never saw Mary so beautiful as on this evening. She was so gentle and beautiful. On this day, She wore the most beautiful gown I have ever seen in my life. Her gown and also her veil and crown had gold and silver sequins of light.
>
> There were two angels with Her. They had the same clothes. Our Lady and the angels were equally beautiful. I don't have words to describe this. One can only experience it.
>
> Our Lady asked me if I had some wish. I told Her I would like to see my earthly mother. She smiled, nodded Her head and told me to stand up. I did and my mother embraced and kissed me and said: "My child, I am so proud of you." Then, she kissed me and disappeared.
>
> After that, Our Lady said to me: "My child, this is our last meeting. Do not be sad because I will come to you on every anniversary (June 24th) with the exception of this year.
>
> Dear child, do not think you have done something wrong and that this is the reason I will not be coming to you anymore. No, you did not. With all your heart, you have accepted the plans which my Son and I had and you have done nothing wrong. No one on earth has received the grace which you and your brothers and sisters have.
>
> Be happy because I am your Mother who loves you with Her whole heart. Ivanka, thank you for your response to My call and of My Son and for preserving and always

remaining with Him as long as He asked you to. Dear child, tell all your friends that My Son and I are always with them when they call Us and ask something of Us. What I have communicated to you about the secrets during these years, reveal to no one until I tell you to." After this, I asked Our Lady if I could kiss Her. She nodded Her head and I kissed Her. Then I asked Her to bless me. She blessed me, smiled and said, "Go, in God's peace." After this She departed slowly, with the two angels. (*The Queen of Peace Visits Medjugorje*, page 214.)

This is a touching and beautiful account of what surely was a difficult occasion for Ivanka. It demonstrates, once again, that the Madonna had come as the universal mother, to gently guide and lead us, yet allow us our freedom of will. By coming in the form of apparitions, she has made her presence and truths known, yet she acknowledges our choice, to accept or reject, using our own free wills.

The apparitions to Ivanka then ceased, with the exception of the promised visits at anniversary occasions and times of need.

That year also brought the announcement of Father Petar Ljubicic as the priest Mirjana had chosen to announce the ten secrets to the world. (See chapter 4, The Ten Secrets.) This announcement was made June 1st.

1986 . . . THE PUBLIC MESSAGES DWINDLE

The Thursday night public messages continued, although the same concepts seemed to be constantly reemphasized. All the messages, which began with detailed exhortations for prayer, fasting, conversion, loving hearts, and peace, at times, were now short and sparse. The Madonna had told the children She had stayed too long, and this was reflected in the ever briefer visitations.

On January 6th, Vicka was told that the Madonna would not appear to her for a fifty-day period and that her visions would resume on February 25th; which they did.

On February 15th at 2:00 p.m., the Holy Mother visited Mirjana, who has not seen daily apparitions since 1982. This was a special apparition, and little is known of its content. It was also in this year, on June 4th, that Mirjana received further information regarding the fulfillment of the first secret.

On June 16, 1986, Ivan left to serve the usual one-year commitment in the Army. His apparitions continued while away from Medjugorje, although little is known about them.

1987: THE MARIAN YEAR

Pope John Paul II had definitely been informed of the events occurring in Medjugorje. It is very interesting that the Pope publicly proclaimed the year 1987 as the Marian Year. During that year, he had also traveled abroad advocating the unity of mankind and his hopes for peaceful coexistence.

Another significant event has also occurred during this Marian Year. The National Directors of the Marian Movement of Priests were together during their annual Retreat-Cenacle in San Marino in early July. On July 3, 1987, while they were still gathered, Father Stefano Gobbi, founder of this movement, received a direct message from the Madonna, Herself. It was an *urgent* appeal, a plea from the heavenly Mother, for us to reawaken our souls . . . before it is too late. (Specifics of this message related in chapter 5, in the section called "Even More Messages.")

Not only had the apparitions changed in terms of frequency and duration, but the nature of the apparitions seems to have changed. What began as a group even, has almost shifted to an individual experience, as each of the young people receives the final secrets. When the last youth has received the last secret, the Madonna has said the apparitions would cease, and shortly thereafter the content of the secrets would be revealed. . . . Over six years ago, a loving invitation to open one's heart to the truth and love of Jesus was extended. Now, an urgent call to conversion was, and is, being issued which remains a constant throughout the messages. Ever present has been Her beautiful permission, as it were, of free will. When the Madonna explained why She had come, and delivered God's truths, it was never in judgment, or with the threat of eternal damnation. Each person, each soul, has been given freedom of choice, has been given the wings, yet fed through the roots. This, in itself, is a beautiful message, though never delivered through Her words. Perhaps we would not be so far from the peace the Madonna is calling us to, if we would begin imitating Her example of living without judgment of those around us, and allowing all people freedom of choice. Indeed, perhaps the reason it is time for Her to go, is that it is time for us to *be* what we can be . . . .

Yet another change in apparition sites came during the Fall of 1987. Since crowds were continuing to form outside the Church in increasing numbers daily, the communist government stepped in. They felt the appearance of the apparitions in the rectory caused too much of a disturbance. The visionaries were moved to the balcony of

St. James Church, where the apparitions still continued daily. Visitors are rarely allowed in the proximity of the visionaries during apparitions, either.

Chapter 3

The Children

The apparitions in Medjugorje are not the first of this kind. It is interesting to note the pattern in church-recognized apparitions wherein children are the visionaries. In Lourdes, France, a single visionary, Bernadette, was fourteen when her apparitions began in January, 1858. At Fatima, Portugal, another site of apparitions which began in 1917, the Madonna appeared to three children: Jacinta, Francisco, and Lucia. In Medjugorje, it is six children.

Apparitions have historically appeared before great global crisis and peril. The number of youths present during an apparition, as well as the frequency of the apparitions, has increased in the last century. One can only speculate on the significance of the increasing frequency of Marian apparitions in this century. Based on the content of the messages delivered to all of the children, it would seem we are living in an age where people have increasingly lost their perspective on the value of the soul, and spiritual development. She is calling us back to our spiritual connection with God. As the Madonna, Herself, has said,

> Dear children: God has allowed me to bring about this oasis of peace. I want to invite you to guard it and let the oasis remain pure always. There are those who are destroying peace and prayer by their carelessness. I am calling you to witness and by your life, preserve peace. Thank you for your response to my call.
>
> —June 26, 1986

WHY CHILDREN?

Why children, indeed! The Holy Mother explains the she has chosen children to consecrate themselves to God and to her Heart. Married people and other adults are often consumed with family and work obligations. Furthermore, children seem less confined by the narrowing attitudes and prejudices that we seem to acquire as we age.

Their minds and hearts seem to be more open vessels for the messages the Madonna has come to reveal; thus, having a capacity to relate the messages with greater clarity than an adult might. Children are uninhibited receptacles of love. As we grow older, many of us lose this receptivity. We become blanketed with anger, fear, and judgmental behavior; our priorities shift. Children, on the other hand, live for the moment. Christ's own words answer the question why children, "I tell you solemnly, unless you change and become like little children you will never enter the kingdom of Heaven. And so, the one who makes himself as little as this little child is the greatest in the kingdom of Heaven." (Matthew 18:3)

Who are these children?

In his book *Queen of Peace, Echo of The Eternal Word,* Father Tomislav Pervan, pastor of the church in Medjugorje, related an experience of an Austrian pilgrim at the moment of the apparition.

> We prayed with the visionaries, each one of us in his own language. Suddenly, the youths fell silent and knelt down. Vicka was kneeling within my narrow field of vision in such a matter that her face, several feet away, was level with my eyes. I can describe only inadequately what her face reflected during the minutes of the apparition. It will remain unforgettable for the rest of my life. She was listening with profound attention. Her face displayed an expression of total self-abandonment and a devotion which absorbed her whole being. Suddenly an expression, resembling a joyous surprise, appeared on her face and her lips formed inaudible words. It was completely silent in the chapel. I could not take my eyes from Vicka. Never before have I seen more beauty in a face, and that on a person who did not stand out among others as being particularly beautiful. I felt as though I were capturing, as if through a mirror, a beauty which does not exist in this world . . . . There have been more important days in my life . . . but I received my profoundest experience in Medjugorje. (pages 11 and 14)

Father Pervan goes on to write personally:

> If, with appropriate justification, apparitions are described as a reflection of the Eternal Light, the visionaries' faces display something of this Eternal Light according to the testimony of

many people who have observed them during the apparitions. (page 14)

These select children of Medjugorje are really no different than any other children of the world. They are still very normal, typical children, except for the fact that through their intense experiences, they have committed their lives to God. Aside from their spiritual focus, the youths each have rather normal interests, and are quickly absorbed by these interests and related projects, which they rarely have in common. It is said that individual personality characteristcs are not discouraged by the Holy Mother, but encouraged. When these apparitions began, the ages of the children ranged from ten (Jakov) to seventeen (Vicka). Now, in 1988, these "children" range in age from seventeen to twenty-four. They all seem to be of average intelligence, except for Mirjana, who is quite exceptional.

The children are as different as one flower from another, yet they remain firmly united in their commitment to the Madonna. Despite intense pressures of all sorts, the seers and their families have withstood all affronts. They believe that the Madonna's authority respects their freedom. Friction within this group is unheard of. They do not argue among themselves, nor is jealousy or rivalry evident. They all have a great respect for each other. As we all know, a deep respect for other children is quite rare in youngsters. Their conviction concerning the truth of the messages is unparalleled.

These young people each fast at least twice a week. With all the Madonna's recommendations, they remain unswerving in their devotion and commitment. They will not even drink black coffee, as some others do on fasting days, for added energy. On the eve of feast days, the seers also fast, and partake of only dry bread and water. The religious community now follows their examples, and has learned the value of fasting.

Each child dialogues with the Madonna in his or her own way. She has always been very understanding and accepts them unconditionally, as any good mother would. Rather than dictate, force, or demand, the gentle Holy Mother counsels and advises. The visionaries seriously consider Her wishes, but don't commit to what they can't do. There is no collective commitment, rather personal decisions based on individual maturity and faith. Each intellectually and from the heart analyzes a challenge, then prays for clarity. Although they have a common mission, each youth has also been called to personal goals.

When the Madonna imparts a message for all of the children, each youth hears the message simultaneously. If the message is of a personal nature, only the child concerned receives the message. Through this form of instruction, the Madonna can best address personal weaknesses, suggest corrective measures, and provide additional personal guidance. When this occurs, the other children never question the one receiving the message. Often, though, the seer's later reaction and expression speak for themselves. Vicka summarizes the Madonna's manner, "Our Lady is a Mother; she loves us all. She will never reprimand anyone or shout at them. She is not at all strict. Her voice, her tender mother manner incite one to pray." (*Medjugorje Unfolds, Mary Speaks to the World*, page 31.)

The Madonna has elected to function as their spiritual director. These children have given their lives to Her. They have not only been called to personal holiness, but to guide others on this path of commitment, as well.

How many of us could maintain an ongoing, totally consistent tale with great embellishments, for over six years, over 2,000 days . . . with five other people . . . and absolutely no deviation?

So, who are these children, who through their actions, reactions, and simple words, have touched literally millions of people from all over the world? They are simple, humble, and honest people, who did not ask for these extraordinary events, yet accepted them joyfully, with all their attendant burdens and persecutions.

VICKA IVANKOVIC

Vicka, the oldest of the group, was born on July 3, 1964. If any one of the six could be considered a leader, it would be Vicka (although none *will* assume a leadership role). Vicka is the most outspoken, and the extrovert of the group. It is interesting, that when the apparitions began, Vicka was the one who was forbidden to speak about them. Her mother and grandmother were afraid that the family would become the brunt of jokes, and be considered crazy. That fear obviously changed later!

Vicka is of average height, and thin for her size. She is very expressive, exhibiting the strength of her conviction even in her features. The charmer, her twinkling eyes, delightful smile, and energetic personality radiate her sincerity to all.

In 1981, the Madonna suggested that it would not be best to leave little Jakov in Medjugorje, while the older visionaries left the area to pursue their schooling. Vicka, without hesitation, quit school in Mostar and returned to the area. She worked in the tobacco fields and spent as much time as possible with Jakov. Vicka later returned to Mostar to complete her studies in the field of clothing, fabric, and textile at the

Professional Textile School. Eventually, she would like to enter the convent.

Although Vicka, overall, is considered reasonably healthy, she suffers from a benign cyst on the brain, which is inoperable because it rests on a blood vessel. Vicka will not ask the Madonna to heal her, although the pain is often intense. Many offers have been made to finance a visit to a specialist, but the young lady has declined these, graciously, saying that she prays daily that God's will be done, and has faith that it is so.

Vicka is one of the last to receive each secret. This certainly should be no stigma, as she has been entrusted with other duties also. When asked about this, it has been reported by some, she responded, "I'm not slow, the Madonna is taking Her time with me." On April 24, 1986, Vicka received the ninth secret, within the confines of her own room.

Vicka has received the gift of prophetic vision from the Holy Mother. The future of our world, and its potential ruin, has been shown to her to emphasize the importance of prayer and its tremendous power to change probable events. Vicka is also the one with whom the Madonna has entrusted the story of Her life. The last details of this biography were being given to Vicka in 1985.

In an interview with Lucy Rooney, SND and Robert Faricy, SJ, recorded in *Medjugorje Unfolds, Mary Speaks To The World,* (pages 30-31.), Vicka describes how the experience of the apparitions have affected her personality,

> Compared with what I was before, I like to pray—and I see that I am praying properly—from the heart. But I can't leave people aside. One has to be involved.

When asked if the Madonna has taught her to pray, Vicka responded,

> Of course she did! But I had to put some effort into learning. Our Lady often repeats that there is no need to wait for Her to say everything, but that we should begin doing something. She wants to see that you are making some effort and that you are willing to pray. You don't have to wait for a message from Our Lady, or stop there and say, "Our Lady has given me a message—finish!" I, and all of us must practice the message. How can I hand it on to you if it only remains words?

MIRJANA DRAGICEVIC

This second oldest of the seers was born March 18, 1965. Mirjana has been called, by some, the most intelligent of the visionaries and studies agronomy at the University of Sarajevo. Mirjana's immediate family, including her younger brother, also live in Sarajevo. Her father is an x-ray technician and her mother, a factory worker.

Born in Bijakovici, Mirjana spends her summer vacations with her grandmother, who still resides there. While visiting, Mirjana was present during the very first apparition. She was also the first to receive all ten secrets from the Madonna on December 25, 1982. Since that time, the Madonna no longer appears to Mirjana daily. Mirjana was told, "Now you will have to turn to God in faith like everyone else; I will appear to you on your birthday, and when you encounter difficulties in life." (*Medjugorje Unfolds, Mary Speaks to the World,* page 94.) Mirjana has recieved a few messages from the Madonna since 1982, in support of the heavy burden of the secrets. In 1985, six messages were received during the summer and transmitted via locutions. She simply heard the Madonna and did not see her. On August 15, 1985, Mirjana received the following message:

> My angel, pray for unbelievers. They will tear their hair. Brother will plead with brother. They will curse their past godless lives and repent. But it will be too late. Now is the time to do what I have been calling them to do these past four years. Pray for them. (*The Queen of Peace Visits Medjugorje,* page 231.)

From the Holy Mother, Mirjana also received an understanding of the state of the Church. During an interview on January 10, 1983, with Father Vlasic, Mirjana said, "The Madonna told me that I should tell the people that many in our time judge their faith by their priests. If a priest is not holy, they conclude that there is no god. She said, 'You do not go to church to judge the priest, to examine his personal life. You go to church to pray. . . .' " ("Miracle at Medjugorje," page 3.) Mirjana continued to explain that many fall from faith, merely due to the "humanness" of the priest. Intentions and motives for prayer were also emphasized in Mirjana's lessons. Purity of the heart and a complete faith in God, knowing that everything is in Divine order, is essential.

Once describing Our Lady, she said, "I can touch her. . . . At the beginning, I looked on Her as something inaccessible, but now, when She is with me, I look on Her as a Mother, as my best friend, who helps me." (*Is the Virgin Mary Appearing at Medjugorje?,* page 48.)

MIRIJA PAVLOVIC

Mirija's sister, Milka, was one of the first children to see the Holy Mother the first day of the apparitions. As fate would have it, on the second day, the skeptical Mirija was to become one of the group of six. Born April 1, 1965, Mirija, the third oldest of the visionaries was studying in Mostar to be a hairdresser. In appearance, she would certainly fit in unobtrusively with a group of American teenagers.

Mirija is said to be the most deeply spiritual of the children. She has been described as "just beautiful" because of her spiritual nature and humility. She has been called on more than any of the others to pray and has risen to the call. Mirija has been entrusted with the responsibility of transmitting many messages to pilgrims, priests, the Bishop, and the Pope. Mirija also received two specific messages for the Pope; one to encourage continued focus on peace, and another, to emphasize the urgency of the messages in light of the potential world scenario. Being a member of several prayer groups, Mirija relates most messages for the parish, as well. She generally delivers the Thursday night public messages. Speaking about prayer, Mirija said, "I gladly say a rosary, but I think nevertheless that I prefer to meditate. I like every sort of prayer, but preferably I read some verses from the Bible, and then I meditate." (*Medjugorje Unfolds, Mary Speaks to the World,* page 35.)

Imagine the responsibilities these visionaries assume! They were merely youngsters when they received this extraordinary title at very tender, developing ages. Many have asked these children for personal favors and blessings. The seers take each request seriously. In Mirija's words, "Many people come with big problems, and after they have told me those problems, I feel uneasy, but they have relaxed. Somehow it all remains in me. Afterwards I try to offer it to God—all the problems of those people—because I know that once I offer it to God, it will not remain in me. But sometimes I still think about those things—it is like a film, passing before my eyes. But when I really offer God everything without reserve, then I feel silence in the depth of my heart." (*Medjugorje Unfolds, Mary Speaks to the World,* pages 35-36.)

IVAN DRAGICEVIC

Although Ivan, the oldest of the boys shares the same last name as Mirjana, the two are not related. Born on May 25, 1965, Ivan is by far, the quietest of the visionaries. He is very serious. Ivan usually appears pensive. He has experienced much difficulty adapting himself to the attention he has received. Once a loner, he can no longer be. Ivan is a very patient soul, and radiates his inner peace and security, in spite of his predisposition. Ivan is known for his politeness, his solid piety, and his disarming honesty and tact. He is very straightforward, not evasive in the least.

In August, 1981, Ivan entered the seminary in Dubrovnik. Knowing that he was having difficulty adapting, the Madonna told him that She would not appear to him until he became accustomed to his new environment. Also, because of his new schedule, Ivan could not be in prayer during the visits to the others. Seven days later, the Madonna resumed her visits with Ivan, but at 2:00 p.m. daily, to accommodate his schedule. Unfortunately, Ivan had not been adequately prepared by his previous education in Medjugorje. He left the seminary and returned home. He was studying on his own and taking correspondence courses. Ivan still wants to become a Franciscan, and hopes to return to the seminary in the future. On June 16, 1986 Ivan joined the Army for the customary commitment of one year.

An insight into Ivan's personality is gained from his response to the question, "What did you do when the others didn't believe?" Ivan stated, "I would have preferred that they believe but, if they didn't want to, that was their personal affair." (*Is the Virgin Mary Appearing at Medjugorje?,* page 49.)

IVANKA IVANKOVIC

Ivanka, the youngest of the girls, was born April 21, 1966. It was Ivanka who first saw the Holy Mother. She is the only one of the seers who has not committed herself to a religious life, as the Madonna encouraged. Ivanka always planned to marry. In Ivanka's words, the Madonna said to the seers, "If you should wish to become nuns, that would be my wish as well. But if you do not wish it, then it is better not to do it." (*Is the Virgin Mary Appearing at Medjugorje?,* page 58.) In 1986, Ivanka married. The Holy Mother did not discourage Ivanka from marriage and was, indeed, pleased with her decision. Ivanka and her new husband now work together in a restaurant(?) in Medjugorje.

Ivanka's mother died in May, 1981, only one month before the apparitions began. Ivanka asked the Madonna about her mother on several occasions. Although her mother was not a devout woman, the Madonna has assured Ivanka that she is well, and with her. Ivanka's father works in West Germany. Her aged grandmother has cared for the family since the death of the mother. She lives in Mostar with Ivanka's brother and sister. The family spends their vacations in Bijakovici, where they cultivate the family farm.

Ivanka received the tenth secret on May 6, 1985. The next day the Madonna appeared to her and said that Ivanka would only see her annually in the future, on the anniversary of the first apparition, June 24th. She also asked Ivanka if she had a wish. Ivanka responded that she wanted to see her earthly mother. The Madonna smiled and Ivanka's mother appeared. "Our Lady told me to stand up. I did and my mother embraced and kissed me and said: 'My child, I am so proud of you.' Then, she kissed me and disappeared." (*The Queen of Peace Visits Medjugorje,* page 214.) Since that date, Ivanka has only seen the Madonna infrequently. The tenth secret is yet to be revealed to the four remaining youths.

JAKOV COLO

Jakov is the youngest of the visionaries. Born June 3, 1971, his mother died when he was two. He rarely sees his father, who works in Sarajevo. Jakov lives with his Uncle Pavlovic, the brother of his deceased mother. His interests include soccer, music, and playing the harmonium.

Jakov has been described as a very lively and mischievous boy. One could even describe his youth as fidgety, which adds to the intrigue in the authenticity of the apparitions. Since Jakov was only ten when the apparitions began, it is difficult to believe that this very active youngster could be still for several hours of prayer and meditation daily. Yet, such is the case, not for a period of months, but for over six years! When questioned about prayer in an interview, Jakov said, "Prayer is never difficult for me. Sometimes, particularly when there are many people coming here, I get distracted. But I try to be patient. Prayer is the most precious thing to me in my whole life . . . . I think that every prayer is a conversation with God—from heart to heart." (*Medjugorje Unfolds, Mary Speaks to the World,* page 33.) In describing a typical day, Jakov responded, "It's like this: when I wake up in the morning I pray a bit, then when it is time, I go to school. In school I do everything on the program. When classes finish I pop into church, at least sometimes. When I come home, and also during the day, I pray. If my aunt needs help, I help her, but if there is nothing, I go out to play. When the time comes to go to church, I prepare myself," (*Medjugorje Unfolds, Mary Speaks to the World,* page 32.) Can life really be this simple, with prayer as a focus? These children *live* the answer.

Jakov also is quick-witted. In a conversation with the Bishop of Mostar, in which Jakov was questioned about the secrets, he replied that they were not yet permitted by the Madonna to talk about them. The Bishop responded, "Well you could write the secrets on a piece of paper, put them in an envelope and leave the envelope here." The youngster immediately retorted "Yes, but I could also write the secrets down, put them in an envelope, and leave the envelope at home."

(*The Queen of Peace Visits Medjugorje,* page 4.)

THE OTHER TWO

A year and a half after the apparitions began in Medjugorje, two more seers surfaced. These two young girls receive the Madonna's messages in a different way, through inner locutions. They "hear" Her words in their hearts, thus, seeing with the eyes of the soul. Although they receive guidance in this manner, both girls have also seen the Holy Mother with their "physical" eyes, too.

These two are not privy to the secrets the other six are receiving. These girls have been given instructions in the truths of the faith, in a much more intimate, personal way. They have been guided to experience and teach personal holiness. A greater reflectiveness and inner experience seems to result from locutions.

In December, 1982, ten-year-old Jelena Vasilj started hearing voices. Perplexed, she would look around to see who was talking. Nobody was. Upon asking someone a question, a voice within her would respond with the correct answer. By the end of December, she heard the same voice calling her to prayer and penance, daily, for seven days. Jelena later said that she knew the voice was her guardian angel's. On December 29th, the Madonna, Herself, spoke with Jelena.

Soon thereafter, the Holy Mother appeared to Jelena daily, sometimes up to three times! Initially, the Madonna came to Jelena in her room, at home. Jelena had received the gift of communicating to the Madonna at will, but she only receives answers to questions of a spiritual nature. When asked about the guidance she receives, Jelena simply replied, "Nothing special . . . . Our Lady just tells me that every Christian should try to be holy." (*The Queen of Peace Visits Medjugorje,* page 96.) She responded to this question with great humility, as the Madonna has imparted many specific lessons to her.

Jelena began receiving her spiritual teachings on May 1, 1983. She was told by the Madonna to write them, as they were to be given to the Church authorities at a later time. By the end of May, Jelena was instructed to advise the priest that a parish prayer group was to be formed. The rules and guidelines for the sanctification of its members were to be received and related by Jelena. The Madonna expected each member of this group to pray at least three hours per day; at least one-half hour in the morning and evening, plus other times throughout the day. She recommended daily Mass. A decision concerning their lives' vocations was not to be made for four years. All members were to renounce everything, including fear, and abandon themselves to God. The Madonna requested that they fast on bread and water two times per week. If problems occurred, they were to fast and pray more. The group was to meet weekly.

It is interesting that Jelena an Marijana are not members of this group, which currently meets Tuesday, Thursday, and Saturday nights in the basement of the Church. They simply function as guides, receiving the teachings and instructions which are later related to the group.

Soon after the group was formed, the Madonna taught:

Now, when a person decides to follow God totally, Satan comes along and tries to remove that person from the path on which they have set out. This is the time of testing. He will try by all means to lead you astray. Satan will tell you: this is too much. This is nonsense. You can be Christians like everybody else. Don't pray, don't fast. I tell you, this is the time when you must persevere in your fast and your prayers. You must not listen to Satan. Do what I have told you. Satan can do nothing to those who believe in God and have totally abandoned themselves to him. But you are inexperienced and so I urge you to be careful. (*The Queen of Peace Visits Medjugorje,* page 99.)

In 1985, Jelena began having "exterior" visions of the Madonna. When she first saw the Holy Mother, she exclaimed, "You are so beautiful!" The Madonna replied, "I am beautiful because I love. If you want to be beautiful—love." (*Medjugorje Unfolds, Mary Speaks to the World,* page 70.)

MARIJANA VASILJ

Marijana and Jelena are very good friends, although they are not related. The first time Marijana saw the Madonna, was in Jelena's home, on March 19, 1983. Marijana saw a white cloud that disappeared when the Madonna became visible.

Marijana and Jelena share the same gifts. They pray daily together, along with a third friend. They do not receive identical messages, but they are usually similar. Currently, Marijana is sharing Jelena's duties of guiding the parish prayer group. The Madonna primarily speaks to Marijana about conversion of others, and the importance of prayer. Marijana seems to receive messages relative to teaching the connection and how conversion can easily be achieved . . . through prayer and fasting. When asked whether the Madonna told Marijana how to pray, she responded, "You must desire to pray." (*The*

Queen of Peace Visits Medjugorje, page 102.)

The children all seem to get along quite well with one another, which in itself in unusual, as any mother would confirm! That they have remained such a close-knit group, with stories that never deviate with any significance from one another, over the past six years, is remarkable. Through their behavior and deeds, it is evident that all these young people are totally devoted to the Madonna and Her messages. Doubt or fear is unknown to these youths. Father Tomislav Ulasic affirmed that the visionaries are ready to "die for Mary and the apparition." (*The Queen of Peace Visits Medjugorje,* page 46.)

As we will see in chapter 5, on messages, the Madonna's primary message to the world is that of prayer. Through prayer one nourishes and sustains their Divine connection, and can avert the challenges contained within the unrevealed secrets.

Chapter 4

Signs and Wonders

Miracles are only miracles because we don't think they can happen

Anonymous

SIGNS AND WONDERS OF HER LOVE

My first experience with the signs and wonders associated with Medjugorje actually occurred on the first day of my visit. Jackie Bailey encountered a lovely, spiritual nun from New York who had seen the Holy Mother on a cloud that day. She shared the experience with Jackie, who then excitedly related it to me. We both heard several people discussing the Miracle of the Sun with great excitement, though as yet, we had not had a direct experience ourselves.

Phenomena like the Miracle of the Sun, the cross spinning at Krizevak, sky writing, and many others are reported to occur daily. Although many of the signs are distinct, there are many which are subtle, almost as if they are indeed omens, pointing us, or directing us forward, that we may continue to find our own way on our spiritual journey.

It was the Madonna herself who smiled lovingly, when Ivanka pleaded during the first week of the apparitions to perform an explicit sign validating the children's experiences to a disbelieving community. There is a haunting simplicity, yet paradoxical complexity in such a response. The infinite wisdom of true knowledge, which the soul and the spirit owns, comes from individual experiences and "learning" the truth. Truth is not dogmatic proof, that perhaps the mind can accept, while the heart strays further from its home. This is not to discredit a discriminating intellect, but the intellect must integrate with the whole being. We *must* remember what we seem to have side-stepped in our new high-tech era: that the heart, mind, soul, spirit, and body must work cohesively together, not as separate entities.

There are many signs, wonders, and miracles which have occurred and been documented in Medjugorje. I have selected the most prominent signs witnessed, as they are the wonders most frequently seen by visiting pilgrims, including myself in some instances. As I continued to personally witness these magnificent wonders, they became a very deep part of my own experience, which I could not deny.

FROM SILVER TO GOLD

I remember when I had the honor of being chosen to enter the room of apparitions. Many converged outside St. James rectory that Easter week, waiting and hoping to be one of twenty selected to enter the room. After several hours of waiting, the select twenty entered the room of apparitions. Clenched in my hand was the white-beaded rosary with it's thin silver chain, that Jim Bailey had given me for Christmas—the key which had prophetically led me to this tiny crowded room. As I waited in anticipation for the visionaries, I recognized a young girl I had seen on the plane.

As the visionaries entered, there was a hush in the room. Suddenly, it was very quiet. I was praying the rosary silently, when I heard a strange voice, as if over a P.A. system saying, "Hail Mary full of grace." As I heard this voice, I saw the visionaries simultaneously drop to their knees. I looked around and realized there was no one speaking in the room. I don't know where that voice came from! I held my rosary beads very tightly, and there were now little pink lights in the beads.

After leaving the church, my friend Jackie mentioned that the little girl I had seen on the plane and in the room of apparitions, had had an experience. The chain linking her rosary beads had turned from silver to gold whenever a decade of Hail Mary's was recited. As she was relating this to me, Jackie looked down, and in surprise, exclaimed that the chain of my rosary was now gold.

Later, I shared the events with the other visitors of the household. I was told that a change in metals had been known to occur; that it was a response to the beautiful energy in the room. I thought this was a simple, but rather appropriate explanation. I was told that it was one of the signs that many pilgrims have experienced.

THE BURNING BUSH

On October 28, 1981 an isolated incident occurred, which hundreds of people witnessed. A bush on the Hill of Apparitions spontaneously ignited. The communist guards rushed to the top of the hill to put the fire out, but by the time they arrived, the fire was gone. Furthermore, there was no evidence of charring or any burnt material in the area where the bush was seen burning. When I discussed this with our interpreter, he informed me that some communists turned in their party membership cards as a result of this and other miracles and visions they had witnessed at Medjugorje.

THEIR FAITH SHALL HEAL THEM

There have been numerous reported healings at Medjugorje. Fifty-six have been documented by Father Rupcic in his book. Physical healings relate to eye and ear diseases, arthritis, vascular problems, neurological disease, wounds, tumors, and a plethora of others. The strength to overcome addictions and smoking, after repeated attempts, has been documented. Psychological healings have also been reported.

Various modes of healing have been identified. Many have occurred at Mass, through the Eucharist (the intake of the body and blood of Christ through communion), while people were making the Way of the Cross, and at the blessing of the sick with the Blessed Sacrament. No, the healings are not limited to religious ceremony. Some have reported healings, attributing them to the simple task of merely opening their hearts. The Madonna, Herself, acquiesces power to the greatest force. In Her own words to the seers, "I cannot heal; only God can." The modes of healing are as different as the individual involved. There is one common thread among all the healings, though, that being faith.

On June 29, 1981 the visionaries specifically asked the Madonna for the healing of a two-and-a-half-year-old boy, who was mute and unable to walk. Jakov reported her response: "Let them (his parents) believe firmly, and he will be healed." (*Is the Virgin Mary Appearing at Medjugorje*, page 28.) Later that evening, as the family of the boy, Daniel, was on their way home, they stopped at a restaurant. The mute little boy banged on the table and said, "Give me something to drink!" (*The Queen of Peace Visits Medjugorje*, page 84.) As time passed, Daniel started standing, then walking. He has even been seen running. The faith was essential—the complete healing, in its own time.

It must be remembered, though, the most frequent and least obvious healings are the spiritual ones. I, personally, don't know how anyone can experience Medjugorje and not receive healing of some sort. After all, love is healing, and in Medjugorje love is everywhere, in many forms.

THE BRILLIANT LIGHT

The appearance of light, with no visible source, assuming many forms, sometimes subtle, sometimes intensive, has been a recurring sign which millions have witnessed, either privately and/or publicly. The first unusual light was seen the third day the Holy Mother appeared. A brilliant light flooded the village and surrounding countryside. Everyone noticed it. The Holy Mother, then, immediately appeared to the children. The next day, the same phenomenon occurred; again, immediately preceding the Madonna's visit. After that day, rarely did others see the light which consistently signals the Madonna's forthcoming presence to the children. During those early visits, the six seers simultaneously saw three flashes of brilliant light, which immediately preceded the Madonna's visits. Later, only one light was seen by the visionaries, but out of this light always came the Holy Mother. After her farewell, she has consistently departed as she came, enveloped in luminescence.

How appropriate that She, who has come as a light, to show us light, precedes her visit with light. Even as a candle is used to light another, it loses none of its power. As long as it shines, it has the infinite capacity to light still another. When Christ said, "You are the light of the world" (Matthew 5:14-16) he was telling us we can be sources of light, as well.

Many people have also seen globes of pure light in the sky at various times. Some report white globes; some see colors. A few people mentioned seeing beautiful lights surrounding the visionaries, primarily around their heads and shoulders. Still others, as I did, saw lights, with no apparent source, in the room of apparitions. The prevailing theme of light, with its unique power, envelops Medjugorje—in totality.

> A city built on a hilltop cannot be hidden. No one lights a lamp to put it under the measure, they put it on the lampstand where it shines for everyone in the house. In the same way your light must shine in the sight of men, so that, seeing your good works, they may give praise to your Father in Heaven. (Matthew 5:15-16)

THE CROSS SPINS AT KRIZEVAK

The cross at Krizevak, itself, is considered by many to be a miracle. The fifteen-ton concrete cross was constructed by the villagers themselves, in 1933. With an undying commitment, the concrete was hauled, by hand, nearly 1800 feet up the rocky and rugged mountain. After completion, the name of the mountain was changed from

Sipovac to Krizevak, Kriz being Croatian for cross. Apparently, flooding was a problem in the area before the cross was constructed. After the construction of the cross, the flooding ceased.

The most recurrent phenomenon in Medjugorje has been observed in the vicinity of Mt. Krizevak, primarily involving the cross, itself. It has been seen at various times of day and also during diverse weather conditions. Hundreds of people have witnessed the mammoth concrete cross spin so quickly, that it seems to become a white column of light, almost like a bridge between the heavens and earth. Visiting pilgrims, as well as locals, have reported that while viewing the cross, it transformed into a brilliant white form of a young lady, which is remarkably similar to the description of the Holy Mother the visionaries have, themselves, seen.

Still others have seen the horizontal crossbar and the lower section of the Krizevak Cross radiating a brilliant white light. It then transformed into a "woman of light." This phenomenon was first observed on October 21 and 22, 1981, the dates Father Jozo was tried and convicted for fostering sedition. The crowd was mesmerized for over thirty minutes. It has been seen several times since these dates, but the duration of the sighting has been much shorter.

MIR—A MIRROR OF PEACE IN THE SKY

On August 6, 1981 the word MIR, meaning peace, was written in large letters across the sky, above Mt. Krizevak with its cross visible in the foreground. It was witnessed by thousands. It has also been seen several times since then, and is a beautiful manifestation of one of the Madonna's most important messages.

Also, painted on the sky as if it were a canvas, a star show has appeared occasionally. Ordinary stars, in their normal positions, have been seen revolving in the sky. As if that wasn't enough, these same stars alternately turned on and off, like strobe lights, for over an hour. This occurred on June 18, 1982 and June 19, 1982, the Feasts of the Sacred Heart and Immaculate Heart, respectively. It was observed again in 1984.

THE MIRACLE OF THE SUN

The Miracle of the Sun, the Dance of the Sun, and the Phenomena of the Sun are all names for the recurring, extremely impressive sight. This sign first occurred in Medjugorje on August 2, 1981, although it was not the first time a sign such as this has appeared to our world. On October 13, 1917, the first recorded Dance of the Sun occurred at Fatima, Portugal. The Blessed Virgin Mary had promised to provide the three children of Fatima a miracle, that She would perform on that day, as evidence of Her existence.

The Miracle of the Sun witnessed in Medjugorje on August 2nd (coincidentally the date of the feast of Our Lady, Queen of Angels within the Catholic Faith) was apparently very impressive. Approximately 150 people observed this marvel, right before sunset, above the Hill of Apparitions. Everyone observed the following sights, without damage to their eyes. The sun appeared to be spinning on its own axis. It also seemed to move toward the observers and then recede. A great darkness loomed behind the sun as the sun moved toward the crowd. Observers didn't know what to think! Many believed it to be Armageddon. Some people panicked, some were afraid, some scampered away, some stayed and cried, and some stayed and prayed. A white cloud, moving down over the hill and toward the sun (which was still spinning), provided the conclusion. Within fifteen minutes, the sky show was over and the sky returned to normal.

The Miracle of the Sun was a deeply personal experience for me, as I'm sure it is for many. I did not see that which was observed, that very first day, of the phenomenon, but what I saw moved me to a greater understanding and respect for the interrelationships of everything. The finest artist could never adequately reproduce the sight that was so graphically sculpted and colored across the sky before my eyes. I was truly in awe. For myself, I experienced a spinning that was almost hypnotic, and I found myself staring at this vortex of gold, seemingly covered by a disc that protected my eyes. It was a pulsating brilliance that defies description. As it spun, it seemed to move towards us, yet still remain in its orbit. It seemed as if it could move in any direction at any given moment. The colors were vibrant fuschia, violet, lavender, silver, and emerald. As soon as one color could be identified, it immediately melted into another, gently blending into its next spectrum.

It is known that staring into the sun for an extended period of time can, and has, damaged the retina in the eyes. Yet, after thirty minutes of staring directly at the sun, my eyes had absolutely no damage to them. Many observers have subsequently had their eyes tested by optometrists. The results have always been the same: no damage, no explanation! I believe this sign, sent from God, was not sent to disturb our vision, rather to enhance it; to help us acknowledge the beauty in our lives, both external and internal. This subtle "sight" is all too often ignored, or forgotten, in the hustle and bustle of daily activities.

Of the thousands, maybe millions of people who have witnessed this marvel, certainly variations would surface. Some have seen not only the spinning sun, but a large heart with six small hearts beneath it (the Madonna and the six visionaries?). Others say they have seen the Holy Mother, with the Sacred Heart, and a herald of angels during their experiences. I'm sure there are other variations, but those are the most frequently reported.

THE TEN SECRETS

> We exhort you to listen with simplicity of heart and honesty of mind to the salutary warnings of the Mother of God . . . not for the purpose of presenting new doctrines, but rather to guide us in our conduct. Pope John XXIII (*The Queen of Peace Visits Medjugorje*, page 137.)

Among the personal counseling and messages for the youths, messages for the villagers, the world, and even the Pope, the most intriguing of all messages are the ten secrets. Why secrets? It is human nature to desire the privilege of knowing a secret. Secrets stimulate interest and arouse curiosity. How better for God to draw and maintain attention on these essential lessons of life? What are these messages? Nobody knows, yet, not even all the children! At this time, only two of the seers, Mirjana and Ivanka (coincidentally the very first two to see the Madonna in Medjugorje) have received all ten progressive and identical secrets. None of the children will share the secrets with anyone else until the Holy Mother permits them to. They continue to resist pressure from authorities and those who are dear to them. Many have tried, using subtle and overt persuasion, with much cunning, and alleging valid reasons, to convince the youths to divulge the information, but to no avail. The children would rather die than violate this confidence; although at rare times they have shared aspects pertaining to these secrets.

When questioned about the secrets' contents, each child replied that they pertain to them, personally, to the community, to the Church, to the world, and to "the sign" (next section). They have shared that only four of the secrets relate to all of mankind. When asked if the secrets concerning the world pertained to good or bad things, their responses were of both . . . good things and bad things. From a taped interview on August 15, 1983, Father Tomislav Vlasic related:

> They (the visionaries) say that with the realization of the secrets entrusted to them by Our Lady, life in the world will change. Afterwards, men will believe like in ancient times. What will change and how it will change, we don't know, given that the seers don't want to say anything about the

secrets. (*The Queen of Peace Visits Medjugorje*, page 139.)

Apparently, the Madonna, Herself, later requested that a report be sent to the Pope. Father Tomislav Vlasic, a Catholic priest, who maintained close contact with the children and won their trust, was asked by Mirjana to execute Her request. Based on information Mirjana related to Father Vlasic on November 5, 1983, a report was prepared. The following excerpt from that report to the Pope, which was sent December 2, 1983, best relates the available information about the secrets:

> According to Mirjana, during the apparition on December 25, 1982, the Madonna confided the tenth and last secret to her, and she revealed the dates on which the various secrets will come to pass. The Blessed Virgin revealed many aspects of the future to Mirjana, many more up to now than to the other seers. For that reason, I relate now what Mirjana told me in a conversation on November 5, 1983. I shall summarize the essential things she said, without any literal quotations.
>
> 1. Before the visible sign is given to humanity, there will be three warnings to the world. The warnings will be warnings on the earth. Mirjana will witness them. Three days before one of these warnings, she will advise a priest of her choice. Mirjana's testimony will be a confirmation of the apparitions and an incentive for the conversion of the world. After these warnings, the visible sign will be given for all humanity at the place of the apparitions in Medjugorje. The sign will be given as the testimony of the apparitions and a call back to faith.
>
> 2. The ninth and tenth secrets are grave matters. They are a chastisement for the sins of the world. The punishment is inevitable because we cannot expect the conversion of the entire world. The chastisement can be mitigated by prayers and penance. It cannot be suppressed. An evil which threatened the world, according to the seventh secret, had been eliminated through prayer and fasting, Mirjana said. For that reason, the Blessed Virgin continues to ask for prayer and fasting: "You have forgotten that with prayer and fasting you can ward off wars, suspend natural laws."
>
> 3. After the first warning, the others will follow within a rather brief period of time. So it is that people will have time for conversion.

Construction continues in Medjugorje.

A simple yellow box where pilgrims mail their letters

Vicka visits daily outside her home with the pilgrims from all over the world.

Throngs of pilgrims gather daily and await a visit with Vicka at her home, located at the foot of Mt. Podbro.

Marija and Jakov in the room of apparitions in the rectory

The visionaries kneel before this cross in the room of apparitions.

The rectory (room to the right), where the daily apparitions have been occurring since April 2, 1985. Pilgrims gather early in the morning hoping to be chosen to go into the room of apparitions in the rectory.

Confessions are heard all day long in many languages in the fields outside the church of Saint James.

St. James Church

Stations of the cross, making the climb up Mt. Krizevac.

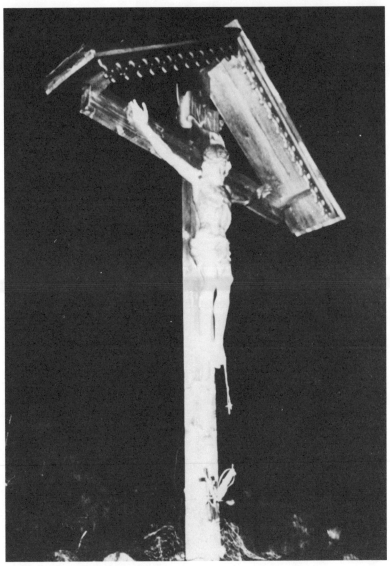

The hill of apparitions (Mt. Podbro) where the Holy Mother first appeared to the children

A late night prayer visit to Mt. Podbro

Author (left) and Vera (hostess) at home in Medjugorje

The author (left) and the matriarch at home in Medjugorje

The path up the hill to Mt. Podbro, site of the first apparitions

4. This time is a period of grace and conversion. After the visible sign, those who are still alive will have little time for conversion. For that reason, the Blessed Virgin calls for urgent conversion and reconciliation.

5. The invitation to prayer and penance is destined to ward off evil and war and above all to save souls.

6. We are close to the events predicted by the Blessed Virgin.

7. Convert yourselves as quickly as possible. Open your hearts to God. This is a message to all mankind. (*The Queen of Peace Visits Medjugorje*, pages 138-139.)

The Holy Mother began conveying the secrets in the early days of the apparitions. Mirjana was the first to receive all ten. Ivanka received the tenth secret on May 6, 1985. Both Mirjana and Ivanka received a paper-cloth-like substance directly from the Holy Mother. The fabric is unlike anything known on this earth, and is indestructible, even by fire. All ten secrets are written, with specific dates (to the minute), on this material. Only the recipient of this substance can read the information it contains. Mirjana cannot read Ivanka's, and vice versa—fascinating! The Holy Mother has told each girl to give their "gift" to a priest of each's choice ten days before the secrets are to occur. The priests, through the grace of the Madonna, will then be able to read and announce each secret, and describe it in its fullness, including time and place, three days before the happening. The priests will only be able to read each secret in its appropriate time, and not all ten secrets at once. On June 1, 1985, Father Peter Ljubicic was named by Mirjana to announce the secrets; even before he resided in the area.

There has been no pattern detected as to when each child receives a secret, other than the fact that they are received by each sequentially. The following chart, relating to the timing of each child's understanding of the secrets, might be helpful:

	1983	1985	March, 1987
Mirjana	9	10	10
Ivanka	7	9	10
Vicka	7	8	9
Marija	6	9	9
Ivan	?	9	9
Jakov	?	9	9

As of March, 1987, four children have not received all ten secrets, and nobody, on earth, knows when they will. We do know, though, when the last youth receives the tenth secret, the apparitions will cease, and the secrets will be revealed soon thereafter.

THE GREATEST SIGN OF ALL

Yet to occur is the greatest sign the Madonna has promised to leave, as a permanent mark on Mt. Podbrdo, the sight of the first apparitions. On August 7, 1981, the Madonna promised a special sign for a disbelieving world. On September 4, 1981, She said that the sign would occur when the apparitions ceased. The sign will be visible to all, and many healings and miracles will occur after this sign appears. This information is only available because the Holy Mother has allowed the children to share those aspects of the information. Each visionary knows the date that it will occur, and has been told by the Madonna that there will be many miracles and healings. When Ivanka was asked, "Will the sign appear very soon or later?" She replied, "It will appear at the proper time." (*Miracle at Medjugorje,* page 4.) There will be three warnings issued before the sign appears. After the first warning, there will still be time for souls to convert to acceptance of God. The time between the second and third will be too short for conversions.

Father Tomislav Vlasic described the available information on "the greatest sign of all" in his December 2, 1983 report to the Pope. A lengthy excerpt from that report is in the preceding section.

I believe though, the Madonna's grave words speak for themselves:

This sign will be given for the atheists. You faithful already have signs and you have become the sign for the atheists. You faithful must not wait for the sign before you convert; convert soon. This time is a time for grace for you. You can never thank God enough for his grace. The time is for deepening your faith and for your conversion. When the sign comes, it will be too late for man.

(*Miracle at Medjugorje,* page 2.)

IN CONCLUSION

In my own experience, I was amazed and touched by the number of individuals I personally interviewed and spoke with in Medjugorje who said that they saw the wonders such as the Miracle of the Sun, the spinning cross at Krizevak, and Mary on a cloud. They said that the signs are there, if you need them. The most surprising thing I heard, though, was that almost everyone concluded their statements with the most beautiful thing they saw; which was the thousands of people, from all walks of life, in this small impoverished village, coming together in love. It was very interesting that most of the people I spoke with were not preoccupied with these beautiful wonders that God made available to them through the Madonna's messages. Rather, they were captivated by the love and the peace they felt as they all stood together as one.

I have not included the apparitions, themselves, in this chapter, even though some would think I should do so. It is my belief that the apparitions cannot be separated from the messages, their content, and their urgency, for if we had not strayed so far from our own souls, perhaps all the phenomena would be unnecessary. I believe there is an urgency connected with the apparitions—the messages—that sets them apart from this chapter—thus justifying their own position of prominence. Each soul must, somehow, delve deep within his being to support himself in his own personal understanding of the Medjugorje messages.

Desiderata

"Go placidly amid the noise & haste, & remember what peace there may be in silence. As far as possible without surrender be on good terms with all persons. Speak your truth quietly & clearly; and listen to others, even the dull & ignorant; they too have their story. Avoid loud & aggressive persons; they are vexations to the spirit. If you compare yourself with others, you may become vain & bitter; for always there will be greater & lesser persons than yourself. Enjoy your achievements as well as your plans. Keep interested in your own career, however humble; it is a real possession in the changing fortunes of time. Exercise caution in your business affairs; for the world is full of trickery. But let this not blind you to what virtue there is; many persons strive for high ideals; and everywhere life is full of heroism. Be yourself. Especially, do not feign affection. Neither be cynical about love; for in the face of all aridity & disenchantment it is perennial as the grass. Take kindly the counsel of the years, gracefully surrendering the things of youth. Nurture strength of spirit to shield you in sudden misfortune. But do not distress yourself with imaginings. Many fears are born of fatigue & loneliness. Beyond a wholesome discipline, be gentle with yourself. You are a child of the universe, no less than the trees & the stars; you have a right to be here. And whether or not it is clear to you, no doubt the universe is unfolding as it should. Therefore be at peace with God, whatever you conceive Him to be, and whatever your labors & aspirations, in the noisy confusion of life keep peace with your soul. With all its sham, drudgery & broken dreams, it is still a beautiful world. Be careful. Strive to be happy."

Found in the old Saint Paul's Church, Baltimore; Dated 1692.

Chapter 5

Messages for the World

Nothing can bring you peace but yourself, nothing but the triumph of principles.

Ralph Waldo Emerson

UNIVERSAL MESSAGES

There have been several books written addressing the issue of the messages in Medjugorje. In researching materials for this book, I discovered that most current books on the topic were written by the clergy. The interpretations and translations of the actual messages differ a bit among languages and authors. In an attempt to be as objective as possible in assessing the significance of the various messages, I listed the dates that the messages were delivered, what the specific content was, and then calculated the predominantly recurring messages.

Over 150 public messages were researched, in addition to the available documentation of the private messages. Public messages began March 1, 1984 and continued on a weekly basis until January, 1987. On January 8, 1987, the Madonna said that She would be giving fewer messages, and that they would be given on the 25th of each month.

The message expressed most frequently was prayer. The other predominant messages in their order of frequency are conversion, love, live the message, open your hearts, peace, humility, and fasting.

Identified consistently as key messages in other books, along with peace and prayer, were faith, confession, and Eucharist. Understanding the importance of these topics in the Catholic faith, and being Catholic myself, I believe there is a universality in all the messages that transcends language, religion, or translation barriers. After having been to Medjugorje, having been in the Room of Apparitions, I believe the

Madonna has come as loving mother to all. In Mirjana's words, "The Madonna always stresses that there is but one God, and that people have enforced unnatural separation. One cannot truly believe, be a true Christian, if one does not respect other religions as well. You do not really believe in God if you make fun of other religions." ("Miracle at Medjugorje," page 3.) The Madonna has said that "each individual's religion should be respected, and of course one's own."

It is also interesting to note that each of the public messages begins with "Dear children." Since these are public messages, it would seem she is addressing not only the visionaries, but all the children of the world.

The group of six visionaries has "seen" where our world is heading, and their mission seems to be not only to alert mankind of our world's potential catastrophes, but primarily, what we can (and *must!*) do to avert, or at least minimize future chaos and conflict. The Holy Mother seems to be issuing a different call to the two "new" seers, Jelena and Marijana; one of a very personal and intimate nature, that of personal holiness. Spiritual growth through personal guidance has developed these youngsters into examples for us all. This is why the Madonna, Herself, has assumed their instruction. Being the loving mother that She is; wanting to give the children not only roots, but wings; the Madonna has *always* respected their own free will. She advises, but never requires. Those of us, who are parents, bosses or friends could benefit tremendously from this "message" alone.

Myself? I am not looking for anything out of the ordinary. I am not looking for anything extraordinary. There are certainly people who may pray harder and fast longer, but what I learned from my experience in Medjugorje was so very clear, that God loves each of us unconditionally, that we are all his children, and in His light, we each have the potential to reflect His image, in which we were made. Our souls can reflect His universal love. What better way to nurture and reflect the Light, the Word, than through the simple truths that She is reminding us of: prayer (to strengthen and nurture our connection with God), conversion to God through transformation of our hearts, and finally living that Truth as reflections of love and peace?

I do not claim to have direct access to understanding what the Madonna has said. Each person must discern and understand the message within the confines of his/her own body, heart, and soul. There is a beauty to what She has said, similar to the beauty found in scriptures. Somehow, the messages, the information, transcends time, culture, and space, becoming available for everyone at all times. I think any Truth will always transcend limitations. I hope you will find a place for these messages in your own life, as they have become an intimate part of mine.

. . . PRAY, PRAY, PRAY. . .

(4/19/84, 5/24/84, 6/21/84, 8/23/84, 11/15/84, 3/29/85)

Dear children! You are not aware of the messages which God is sending to you through me. He is giving you great graces and you are not grasping them. Pray to the Holy Spirit for enlightenment. If you only knew the greatness of the graces God was giving you, you would pray without ceasing. Thank you for your response to my call.
—November 8, 1984

Dear children! You do not know how many graces God is giving you. These days when the Holy Spirit is working in a special way. You do not want to advance, your hearts are turned towards earthly things and you are occupied by them. Turn your hearts to prayer and ask that the Holy Spirit be poured upon you. Thank you for your response to my call.
—May 9, 1985

Dear Children! Today I want to call you to pray, pray, pray! In prayer you will come to know the greatest joy and the way out of every situation that has no way out. Thank you for moving ahead in prayer. Every individual is dear to my heart. And I thank all of you who have rekindled prayer in your families. Thank you for your response to my call.
—March 29, 1985

Dear Children: Today I am calling you to prayer. Without prayer you cannot feel me, nor God, nor the graces I am giving you. Therefore, I call you always to begin and end each day with prayer. Dear Children, I wish to lead you evermore in prayer, but you cannot grow because you don't want it. Thank you for your response to my call.
—July 3, 1986

Dear Children: Today I invite you to pray. I give you a special invitation, dear children, to pray for peace. Without your prayers, my dear children, I cannot help you to understanding what my Lord has given me to give you. Therefore, dear children, pray that peace will be given to you by God.

—October 24, 1986

During the first meeting of the Tuesday night prayer group, the Holy Mother said that the group should strive to love their enemies. She also said, "I know that you are not able to love your enemies, but I beg you to pray every day at least five minutes to the Sacred Heart and to my Heart and we will give you the divine love with which you will be able to love even your enemies." (*The Queen of Peace Visits Medjugorje*, page 99.) After recommending that a three-hour per day commitment to prayer be made by all members of this group, the Madonna commented, "You have begun to pray three hours a day and this is good. But, you keep looking at your watches and worrying about the numerous things you will have to do after the meeting. If you continue doing this, you will not be able to fulfill these duties properly nor will you be able to advance spiritually. You must renounce your preoccupations and be ready so that the Spirit can lead and guide you interiorly. Only in this way, can you advance spiritually. When you do this, you will discover that you have the time to complete all your duties and also have time left over." (*The Queen of Peace Visits Medjugorje*, page 99.)

Why should we pray? To pray effectively, we must understand how it works. Our will always executes its desires, whether those desires are conscious, or not. Through prayer, we can define more clearly, or redefine, our aspirations, faith, and will. The power of prayer lies in focusing and aligning our will with God. The goal of prayer, therefore, should be a totally conscious connection with God. The relationship, or connection, has to be developed before the "power" is useful.

How do we know when we've made the connection? A preference for reflection and inner worship is developed when we have truly connected. It is only then that we can begin to fathom personal holiness. One must align thoughts, feelings and behavior with the Divine. Then, slowly, old patterns and inner struggles will begin to dissipate.

If one enters into the act of prayer with fear or doubting of God, an interference, an obstruction, is already present in the relationship. A relationship inhibited with fear or doubt cannot be open and trusting. If you are fearful of someone, or distrustful, that affects your relationship with that person. The fruits of an open relationship evolve from sincere faith and purity of heart. The Madonna told the seers, "You are like water faucets and can become rusty." (*The Queen of Peace Visits Medjugorje*, page 141.) This has been interpreted as a warning by the community; meaning that the focus on personal and spiritual growth, through prayer, is essential for these children (and us) to preserve the clarity of any messages. Joyful prayer is from the heart and rides on a crest of emotion or aspiration. One day, Jelena was reciting the rosary, as she had been taught in church. The Holy Mother said to her, "This is not the rosary. You prayed only with your lips. You must concentrate. You must sit down without moving and enter inside." (*The Queen of Peace Visits Medjugorje*, page 100.) Sincere prayer is very powerful. Mechanical and repetitive prayer becomes insignificant when juxtaposed with sincere prayer from the heart.

There is an urgency in the Madonna's words. She has said so, Herself. The time has come for us to re-establish a waning and thinning friendship with God. Prayer is the concept emphasized in over half of the public messages! It is our link, our communication line with God. Any relationship exists, and is strengthened by the ability to communicate. How can one begin to understand the true essence of peace, of love? How can one begin to live the message until one has opened his heart? The way to becoming better than we are is through prayer, by forging the link. I do not mean the empty repetition of words that have lost their meaning and significance. I mean whatever it is that stirs the heart to a communion with God. Isn't that what prayer really is—a communion with God? Whether it be through reading the Bible, recitation of the rosary, meditation, or merely listening to the sounds of God reverberate through the wind or ocean, all we have to do is listen to that still, small voice within, the echo of the infinite Word. *Ask* Jesus to come in and we are praying. She is urging us, in whatever way we can, to listen and to connect, with our hearts, that they may become open to God's infinite Light. Only then, can we too, become Lightbearers.

CONVERSION

Dear Children! Today I want to tell you to begin to work in your hearts as you would work in the fields. Work and change your hearts so that the spirit of God will move into your hearts. Thank you for your response to my call.

—April 25, 1985

Dear Children: Today I am calling you to open yourselves more to God so that He can work through you. For as much as you open yourselves you will receive the fruits from it. I

wish to call you again to prayer. Thank you for your response
to my call.
—May 6, 1986

Dear Children! I invite you to decide completely for God. I
beg you, dear children to surrender yourselves completely
and you will be able to live everything I say to you. It will not
be difficult for you to surrender yourselves completely to
God. Thank you for your responses to my call.
—January 2, 1986

Dear children: Today I am calling you to give me your heart
so I can change it to be like mine. You are asking yourselves,
dear children, why you cannot respond to what I am seeking
from you. You cannot because you have not given me your
heart so I can change it. You are seeking, but not acting. I call
you to do everything I tell you. In that way I will be with you.
Thank you for your response to my call.
—May 15, 1986

Hand in hand with prayer is conversion. I interpret the message of
conversion as a universal message. Due to the misunderstanding of the
word, and the various interpretations, controversy has arisen. Some
who are Catholic perceive it as a message for nonbelievers; to convert
to their faith. Many non-catholics who perceive it as a call to the Catholic
church disclaim the messages because of this scope. According to
Funk and Wagnall's *College Standard Dictionary*, the theological defini-
tion of conversion is "the act of turning or of being turned from the
supreme love of self to the love and service of God; the spiritual change
by which the soul is turned to God from spiritual indifference or gross
forms of sins." Therefore, conversion is a transformation, a change
from one state of consciousness, or understanding, to another. It is a
turning towards God.

Through prayer and conversion, we, the sons and daughters of
God, the children of the world, have the same access to that Divine
friendship, a vision in the soul, as those six children in Medjugorje. We
must remember, though, that this type of conversion requires a
change in focus, from self to others, and service. This call to conversion
does not preclude those of the Catholic faith. The method of conversion
does not necessarily assume the theology and activity of the sacra-
ments exclusively which applies to Catholics and should be taken
seriously by Catholics.

This simple message is that all people are called, first as individuals, within the privacy of their hearts, to their own devotion to God, in whatever religion or faith they see that truth in. The Madonna has said, Herself, that there are no religions in heaven. Furthermore, Ivanka related, "The Madonna said that religions are separated on the earth, but the people of all religions are accepted by her Son." ("Miracle at Medjugorje," page 4.) Now, what we have is one conversion from the material to the spiritual. Our view of life, and its associated priorities change. Have you ever wondered why some people are so full of joy, or seem to live such fulfilling, complete lives? Look into those people's hearts. It's simply a matter of focus, of perspective, of faith, of love.

OPEN YOUR HEARTS

Dear Children: Everything has its time. Today, I invite you to start working on your hearts. All the work in the fields is finished. You find time to clean the least important places but you left your hearts aside. Work more and with love, clean your hearts. Thank you for your response to my call.
—October 17, 1985

Dear Children! I wish on this Feast Day for you to open your hearts to the Lord of all hearts. Give me all your feelings and all your problems. I wish to console you in all your temptations. I wish to fill you with the peace, joy and love of God.
—June 20, 1985

Dear Children: Once again today I want to invite you to pray. When you pray, Dear children, you become more beautiful. You become like flowers which, after the snow, show forth their beauty, and whose colors become indescribable. And so you, dear children, after prayer before God display everything that is beautiful so that you may become beloved by him. Therefore, dear children, pray and open your inner self to the Lord so that he may make of you an harmonious and beautiful flower for heaven. Thank you for your response to my call.
—December 18, 1986

Dear Children: Today also I am grateful to my Lord for all He is giving me, especially for this gift of being with you again today. Dear children, these are the days in which the Father is giving special graces to all who open their hearts. I am

blessing you. My desire, dear children, is that you may recognize God's graces and place everything at His disposal so that He may be glorified by you. My heart follows all your steps attentively. Thank you for your response to my call.
—December 25, 1986

With our hearts open, we are able to see all facets of life's experience, clearly, and accept them joyfully as what they are, merely lessons. To open our hearts requires us to take a good, long look inside ourselves. When we look at a person, or a situation, or an experience, do we see the beauty, the goodness, the positive aspects? Few of us do, at least consistently! To truly open our hearts, we must often shift our attitudes, our beliefs, our perceptions, and our perspectives. No longer will we find it necessary to be judge, jury, or even executioner. With an open heart, we can become more Christ-like. What I remember most, as I think of open hearts, are Christ's words to a community preparing to stone the harlot: "Let those of you without sin cast the first stone." "Do not judge and you will not be judged; because the judgments you give are the judgments you will get, and the amount you measure out is the amount you will be given. Why do you observe the splinter in your brothers eye, and never take the plank out of your own?" (Matthew 7:1-4)

With an open heart, we can begin to love unconditionally, and it is in love's hand, that peace comes.

LOVE

Dear Children! I am calling you to love your neighbors, to love those people from whom the evil is coming to you and so, in the power of love, you will be able to judge the intentions of heart. Pray and love, dear children. In the power of love you can do even those things that seem impossible to you. Thank you for your response to my call.
—November 7, 1985

Dear Children: I wish to thank you for your sacrifices and I invite you to the greatest sacrifice, the sacrifice of love. Without love, you are not able to accept me or my son. Without love you cannot witness your experience to others. That is why I invite you, dear children to begin to live the love in your hearts. Thank you for your response to my call.
—March 27, 1986

Dear Children: Today I am calling you to a life of love towards God and your neighbor. Without love, dear children, you cannot do anything. Therefore, dear children, I am calling you to live in mutual love. Only in that way can you love me and accept everyone around you. Through coming to your parish, everyone will feel my love through you. Therefore, today I beg you to start with the burning love with which I love you. Thank you for your response to my call.

—May 29, 1986

Dear Children! Hatred creates division and does not see anybody or anything. I invite you always to carry unity and peace. Especially, dear children, act with love in the place where you live. Let love always be your only tool. With love turn everything to good that the devil wants to destroy and take to himself. Only this way will you be completely mine and I will be able to help you. Thank you for your response to my call.

—July 31, 1986

There have been many words written about this short little word. Sometimes, I wonder if all the many words somehow pale when confronted with actions. Too much time is spent talking about love, rather than in the act of loving, itself. I do not mean superficial emotion that is turned on and off like a faucet, which can, indeed, seem "rusty." I mean the kind of love Christ demonstrated throughout His life, the kind of love Ghandi lived, and Mother Theresa of Calcutta is living daily.

Perhaps what the Madonna is saying, after all, is to *live* love. Who better to remind us that actions speak louder than words, than She, who continually lived love, while also witnessing her Son's life, and death? Christ's life and actions are certainly a model for anyone and everyone and I'm sure, very difficult to accept for a mother with human emotions. It is said that Mother Mary, with unconditional love, never wavered or doubted her son's decisions. I might have! What about you? The Blessed Virgin is a perfect example of total love and faith. Again, a shift in perspective is called for here. With true love in one's heart, one has faith, and trust that all is in Divine order. Who are we to second-guess or judge another's decisions or actions. With love, we each have the capacity to totally love another, regardless of actions or behavior we do not understand. That's what we must strive for! By calling us to love, the Madonna is calling us to love unconditionally.

Pope John Paul II has said about love, "Real love is demanding.

Love demands effort and a personal commitment to the will of God. It means discipline and sacrifice, but it also means joy and human fulfillment." (*The Pope in America*, back cover) We all search for joy, happiness, and contentment. Where do we look for these elusive emotions? Too often we seek satisfaction from material "things" or other people. The search for joy, contentment, and fulfillment must begin within our hearts. The Madonna is guiding us to look in a forgotten and often ignored place, within ourselves. Yes, it requires time, and effort, and a personal commitment, but it's well worth it, because the rewards are truly what we seek. After all, if we are truly made in His likeness, then we must find what we are so desperately searching for. Let your light shine!

PEACE

Dear Children: God allowed me to bring about this oasis of peace. I want to invite you to guard it and let the oasis remain pure always. There are those who are destroying peace and prayer by their carelessness. I am calling you to witness and by your life, preserve peace. Thank you for your response to my call.

—June 26, 1986

Dear Children: Through your own peace, I am calling you to help others to see and to start searching for peace. Dear children, you are at peace and therefore, you cannot comprehend the absence of peace. Again, I am calling you so that through prayer and your life you will help destroy everything evil in people and uncover the deception which Satan is using. Pray for truth to prevail in every heart. Thank you for your response to my call.

—September 25, 1986

There are some who cite peace as the central theme of the Madonna's messages. An atmosphere of peace blankets the village of Medjugorje, which was known as an area of conflict and strife before the appearance of the apparitions. Pilgrims universally experience and take home a new feeling of peace. Yes, peace, both internal and global is the ultimate goal. Again, as a good mother would, the Madonna has not merely preached peace; She has given us the tools to actualize peace. She has guided not only the visionaries, but the villagers, through the seers. In the six years that She has been appearing, Medjugorje and its people have transformed into examples for the rest of mankind. It would seem that this, itself, could be the greatest evidence, yet, of Her existence. It is definitely proof of the power of the messages. What better gift to give our world than an example for the rest of us to follow.

By understanding and accepting these gentle lessons, and living our lives in love, wouldn't the natural effect seem to be an inner peace within ourselves? This peace is a subtle serenity, a harmony among all aspects of ourselves. A radiance of this spirit of peace to others becomes the extension of personal (inner) peace. If peace can be achieved in Medjugorje in this manner, why can't it be achieved on a greater scale; even in global proportions?

"Make peace the desire of your heart, for if you love peace, you will love all humanity, without distinction of race, color or creed." (Pope John Paul II, *The Pope in America*, page 35.) World peace can only be achieved when the essence of peace is in the hearts of those with power (yes, we each possess this dormant power). Peace is as soft and quiet as sunshine, yet is as powerful and vital as the noonday sun. When an individual soul desires peace, and draws it into his/her heart, it will become active in their lives. When enough individuals *live* the spirit of peace, peace shall reign upon the earth.

It's very simple, just like the Madonna's message. Each individual can make a difference! If we can live love and radiate this spirit of peace to the people in our lives, peace would not be a global problem, requiring global solutions. It simply becomes an individual issue requiring individual action. Do you see the beauty in the simplicity of individual loving actions and deeds creating world peace?

LIVE THE MESSAGE . . . BE A LIGHT!

Dear Children: Today I am calling you to live in humility all the messages I give you. Dear Children, do not glorify yourselves when living the messages by saying: "I live the messages." If you carry the messages in your heart and live them everyone will realize this, so, there is no need for words which serve only those who do not hear. For you it is not necessary to speak. For you my dear children it is necessary to live and witness by your lives. Thank you for your response to my call.

—September 19, 1985

Dear Children: Today also I want to call you to take seriously and live the messages which I am giving you. Dear children, because of you I have remained this long to help you to put into practice all the messages which I am giving you. Therefore, dear children, out of love for me live all the messages which I am giving you. Thank you for your response to my call.

—October 30, 1986

Dear Children: In your life you have all experienced light and darkness. God gives to each person knowledge of good and evil. I am calling you to the Light, which you have to carry to all people who are in darkness. From day to day, people who are in darkness come to your homes. Give them, dear children, the light. Thank you for your response to my call.

—March 14, 1985

Dear Children: Today I am calling you to decide if you wish to live the messages I am giving you. I wish you to be active in living and transmitting the messages. Especially, dear children, I desire you to be the reflections of Jesus who enlightens an unfaithful world which is walking in darkness. I wish that all of you may be a light to all and witness to the light. Dear children, you are not called to darkness, you are called to light and to live the light in your lives. Thank you for your response to my call.

—June 5, 1986

The quality and merits of the Holy Mother's messages certainly speak for themselves. In light of Her messages, the issue of Her presence seems to quickly fade into the background. Whether we accept her presence, or not, we have free will. The Holy Mother has always respected that in the seers, and in us. She has come as an intercessor, with a mission: the Holy Mother is not only appealing to us, but pleading with us to allow Her to help us realign our focus, our priorities, ourselves, through Her messages. There is absolutely no trace of force, intimidation, or fear in *any* of the messages. Instead, the essence of love prevails throughout—the universal message of love.

It matters not what our values, beliefs, or religious or spiritual affiliations happen to be. We are all children of God. The messages are lessons for us all, so that each of us may experience what we truly desire from life. We have choices. We can make a difference—in our lives and in others.

Now is the time . . .

you CAN . . .

BE A LIGHT!

EVEN MORE MESSAGES

As mentioned previously, on July 3, 1987, an urgent message from the Holy Mother was received through Father Stefano Gobbi, founder of the Marian Movement of Priests. After reading a transcript of this message, and noting the consistency in style and information, a great urgency was again emphasized.

Due to the length of the transcript, only excerpts can be provided here. (Reference bibliography to obtain complete transcript.) The Madonna began this message with, "My beloved sons." She continued, referring to this Marian Year, which Pope John Paul II has pronounced for 1987, saying:

> I have wanted you about my person as a mother who gathers her children together to make to them a recommendation which she has so very much at heart, A VERY LAST RECOMMENDATION FOR YOU, to accompany you on your difficult journey.

> These are the times of my strong admonition. Come Back! Come back, O humanity, so far away and depraved! Come back along the road of conversion and of return to the Lord . . . .

> In all the countries to which you return, you must proclaim and spread this motherly, anxious and urgent message: COME BACK! COME BACK RIGHT AWAY TO THE GOD OR YOUR SALVATION AND PEACE.

> The time that has been granted to you for your conversion is almost over. The days are counted. Come back right away along the road of return to the Lord if you want to be saved.

> I have need that this urgent message of mine immediately reach every part of the earth. YOU MUST BE MY MESSENGERS.

> Iniquity covers the whole earth. The Church is as it were darkened by the spread of apostasy and sin. The Lord, for the triumph of his mercy, must as of now purify you with his strong action of justice and of love. The most painful, most bloody hours are in preparation for you. These times are closer than you think. Already during this year, certain great events will take place, concerning what I predicted at Fatima

and have told, under secrecy, to the children to whom I am still appearing at Medjugorje.

Beloved sons, see along your roads those who are far away, the little ones, the poor, those cast aside, the persecuted, the sinners, the drug addicts, those who are victims of the reign of Satan. I want to save ALL my children. I HAVE NEED OF YOU. I WANT TO SAVE THEM THROUGH YOU.

Yes, after the time of the great suffering, there will be the time of the great rebirth . . . . YOU WILL SEE A NEW EARTH AND NEW HEAVENS . . . . This will be a universal reign of grave beauty, of harmony, of communion, of sanctity, and justice and of peace.

The great mercy will come to you as a burning fire of love and it will be given by the Spirit of Love . . . .

The Holy Spirit—Yes!—will come down like a fire but in a way different from the first Pentecost. It will be a fire which burns and cleanses, transforms, and sanctifies, which renews the earth from its very foundations, which opens hearts to a reality of life and brings souls to the fullness of holiness and of grace. YOU WILL KNOW A LOVE WHICH IS GREATER AND A SANCTITY WHICH IS MORE PERFECT THAN ANY YOU HAVE HITHERTO EVER KNOWN.

NOW YOU MUST GO DOWN TO BE BEARERS OF THIS MY MESSAGE. Bring to every part of the earth this pressing request of mine. Gather all together in the cenacle of my Heart to prepare them to live the awaited vigil of the new times which have now arrived and which are now at your doors.

Do not be discouraged by the difficulties which you find before you. I am your comfort. I am the Mother of your consolation. One by one, I receive you and, together with you, all the souls who are entrusted to you, all those dear to you, all the persons whom you love, all your brothers who are furthest away. Don't forget anyone. Come all together. I am the Mother of all—of all.

Remember, that this message was related after the others, which are messages of *personal* preparation. Don't merely speak these messages, of prayer, of conversion, of love, of peace, and as some would interpret, doom. *Be* these messages! It is through example that we teach best. In the total integration lies our power. Hypocrites are rarely admired.

Science and technology have led us to great achievements in our time. With each technological achievement, though, it seems our priorities shift, ever so slightly. We have definitely polluted our earth, and maybe our minds. We now have air, water, and soil which are toxic to an ever-increasing number of us. These most basic gifts provide our nourishment. And we wonder why we are becoming ill, addicted, or crazy? Is it possible that our body and minds have also become polluted, to the point that maybe we aren't even aware of it?

It is a time for cleansing, of ourselves, and of the earth. The Holy Mother is telling us this. We are shriveling, like flowers without proper light or water. The cleansing of the earth, through events such as earthquakes, volcanos, floods, and other unusual "disasters" would seem inevitable. Erratic weather and the increased frequency of catastrophes is already occurring. It is nothing to fear, merely a consequence of our actions.

The Madonna is pleading with us to change our ways. As She has said many times, this is a time of grace. This is a time when guidance has been given, in hopes that we will *choose* the path which is best for us, as individuals and as mankind. She is telling us that if we only follow Her guidance, we will come to know a greater love than we have ever known. If we do this, there will be no need for concern or fear of earth changes, or Armageddon. The earth and its people must be cleansed, one way or another. If you choose to clean your heart and your lifestyle, you will know peace, whether amidst chaos or not. If chaos is present, you can *be* the light, serve, and witness transformation, yourself!

It's your choice . . . you CAN . . . BE A LIGHT!

Chapter 6

Reflections of a Pilgrim

Pilgrims are God seekers, and in seeking God, they find their true self. We cannot separate the experience of God and the experience of self, for each person bears within himself what makes him or her a personality, an individual unique in the history of creation, the image of the invisible God. In meeting God, the pilgrim meets his own run-away heart.

—Fr. Tomislav Pervan, O.F.M.
Pastor of St. James Church
(*Queen of Peace: Echo Of The Eternal Word*, page 53.)

Dear Friends,

I can only hope that my experiences, shared about Medjugorje will help to change lives for the better, to free people from the illusory bondage which has complicated our lives, and enveloped many of us in misery, fear, guilt, and shame. The Madonna's messages are meant to free us, to be the people that we were intended to be.

It's been close to a year, since I journeyed to Medjugorje, and much has happened. I truly believe I am capable of much more love and compassion for my fellow man. I even surprise myself, sometimes. My vision is clearer, and my life, far simpler. I now understand that God, in His wisdom, hid all the secrets inside us; for He knew it would be the last place we would look.

Isn't this true? We look outside ourselves to what other people think, when we know all the while that we come in alone, and we go out alone. We look to fancy cars and new homes, yet do we take any of this with us? We look to spas and country clubs, beauty treatments and cosmetics, but isn't it true that we ultimately shed the body? "Remember man that thou art dust and unto dust thou shalt return."

It would appear that we are, at times, obsessed with titles and accumulating. Does God even care? Will He ask what we materially possessed? Will He ask if we were president of our corporations, homecoming queen, or president of the garden club?

Or, will He ask how we tended our gardens? Will He take one of the two keys which unlock our hearts, remembering that we hold one of the keys, and see how empty or how full our hearts are? Are we, any of us, prepared to stand before Him at this moment and say we always exercised love; that we have always responded to His call?

It has occurred to me that if I can identify just one whom I do not love, that I am not what I can be; because I am, and you are, made in His image and likeness. It has occurred to me that if there is just one of His people that I do not love, then I am not loving; if there is one that I cannot forgive, then I am not forgiving.

It is amazing how we delude ourselves, amazing how we escape examining our own lives and defer responsibility for this to others! Could it be that we are so caught up in this illusion of life that we never really live it, not realizing that we are on a journey back to God?

Is that why some don't want to hear that God has been perform-ing miracles through the Holy Mother for six years in a remote corner of the communist world? Is that why some don't want to know? Because it's *past* time to get in touch with ourselves and the way we are living our lives?

We can change in an instant, by remember who we really are—children of God. We have a choice. Mary, Herself, has said that She loves us, even when we're far away. She denies not one of us.

So, where do we begin? In our own homes, within the structure of our own families. Mary's cry is a plea for love, a plea for peace. We need only look to the Holy Family for our example.

Can we put aside materialism? Can we give our families, sent to us by God, the love, kindness, patience, and forgiveness that they deserve?

Our suicide rate is a cry for love, a cry for our time, quality time. Anorexia, bulimia are more cries for love and drugs are another cry for love. Children need us; need our time; need our support. What good to profit the world in money and possessions while losing a child entrusted to us? God is not into accumulation, but love. If we live it, we teach it. It is not the knowledge of virtue that sustains us, but the manifestation of it.

A child, of about nine years old, asked me recently how to love an angry peer at school; a child who always said terrible things to everyone. I was surprised that this small child spoke up in a room full of adults. Her question was so bright and applicable to all. How do we love the unlovable? I though for a moment, then responded directly to her.

"Are you made in the image and likeness of God?"

She said, "Yes."

Then, said I, "Do you know how very special you are to be a child of God?"

A simple yes was her response.

"Then, isn't the little girl who abuses you special too? Isn't she also a child of God?"

"Yes," the young girl sheepishly responded.

"Could it be that she has forgotten who she is? If this is true, how could she possibly remember who you are?"

"I don't know," came the meek response.

"It's kind of sad, don't you think?"

"Yes," she responded again.

"So can you love and forgive her?"

"I think so," she said.

I said earlier that life has become quite simple for me. I basically see every problem as a cry for love. I then try to respond accordingly. Certainly we don't want to teach anger, or hatred, or hostility. We have enough of that, don't you think? And, so it gets easier to respond with love. Sometimes, we (with God's assistance) can turn someone around instantly! Other times it's not so easy. But if enough people love, how can fighting occur?

I believe that one day we shall all love, unconditionally. I choose to believe this against all odds, because it gives me peace and joy, as well as hope.

In my own home, during the last year, I have seen my own children come to grips with the fact that everything is in Divine order, that God allows things to happen, allows our choices, that we might learn to see opportunity, not failure; faith and love instead of disappointment or hatred. I feel blessed to be part of this experience, this miracle.

There have been many other experiences, as well, which have served as blessings to me, this past year. A Jewish man, praying the rosary, after a terrible automobile accident, a man who felt the hands of the Holy Mother upon him, and a man who was instantly healed, called to tell me. There are many other stories such as this.

Recently, I spoke to the Carmelites at Epiphany Church in Richmond, Virginia. A nun gave me a photograph of the Holy Mother, taken in the Room of Apparitions in Medjugorje, by an Italian priest from the Vatican. Imagine the priest's surprise when His film was developed. There it was, on the film, a picture of the Holy Mother, reportedly verified as the Holy Mother by the visionary, Marija! Imagine my joy, if you will, upon receiving a copy of this unique picture! My life is now full of joy. Everywhere I go to speak, I hear another story of healing from Medjugorje. I feel the love of those I visit. I feel very humble in their presence. I will continue to take these messages everywhere I'm asked.

The Holy Mother closes her messages with, "Thank you for your response to My call." I now thank all of you for your response to Her call. It seems appropriate to leave you with the prayer of St. Francis:

> Lord make me an instrument of Thy peace; where there is hatred, let me sow love; where there is injury, pardon; where there is doubt, faith; where there is despair, hope; where there is darkness, light; where there is sadness, joy. O, Divine Master, grant that I may not so much seek to be consoled as to console; to be understood as to understand; to be loved as to love; for it is in giving that we receive, it is in pardoning that we are pardoned, and it is in dying, that we are born to eternal life.

God's promise was and remains for *all* His children who live their lives in Him and for Him. For pity's sake, will we awaken to His call, to love and peace which is our Divine inheritance? It's our choice. Choose to BE A LIGHT!

May peace and love be always with you,

Ann Marie Hancock

If the lost word is lost, if the spent word is spent
If the unheard, unspoken
Word is unspoken, unheard;
Still is the unspoken word, the Word unheard,
The Word without a word, the Word within
The world and for the world;
And the light shone in the darkness and
Against the Word the unstilled world still whirled
About the centre of the silent world.

—T. S. ELIOT
Ash-Wednesday

Appendix I

Questions and Responses

Initially, upon hearing the story of your friend Jackie Bailey, didn't you have doubts about what she conveyed, and did you express them? Wasn't it strange that one day someone would come into your home and tell you the Mother of God is appearing in Yugoslavia?

I suppose the source is significant in this experience. Had just anyone come to my home sharing this information, I might have thought he or she had been in the brandied peaches, but I've known Jim and Jackie for years. Jim would be the last person to share such information with me! He had quite obviously had a profound experience that changed his life. You must also remember that he is a hard *news* reporter who took this assignment with reluctance.

Did Jackie share what specifically happened in Medjugorje to change Jim's life? If so, could you describe it?

Certainly. Jim was privileged to actually go into the room of apparitions, which is a tiny priest's bedroom in the rectory of St. James Church. This, in itself, was unusually lucky, since only twenty people are selected from the thousands who make the pilgrimage. Jim was also allowed to film in this room, which is virtually a miracle in itself, given the intense scrutiny and surveillance of the communists. Yet, Jim, with camera in hand, was permitted to film in this special place!

In the room of apparitions, Jim saw what he described as a reflection of little lights in his rosary beads. When he looked for the source, there was nothing which could create this reflection, the lights. He said, simultaneously as this happened, he felt an enveloping sense of peace.

Does everyone pray the rosary there?

In the room of apparitions, the visionaries recite the rosary in Croatian, and those in the room pray with them. The rosary is prayed for about forty-five minutes before the Holy Mother actually appears to the children.

How did you know when the Holy Mother appeared?

After the rosary is prayed, the children move to the center of the small, crowded room, and are directly before the cross. In a synchronized, effortless movement, they drop to their knees. This indicates Her presence.

Do you feel the pilgrimage to Medjugorje is necessary?

We are like blindfolded children in a room full of light! I journeyed to Yugoslavia only to find out that I didn't need to go. My experience in Medjugorje did reawaken in me the understanding that light is within us all; that we each can find God in our hearts and lives every day. The trip further strengthened my faith, and served to remind me of what I already intuitively knew.

You talk about the communists. Can you elaborate on your experience at Zagreb (the airport)?

The stay (delay) at the airport served as a preparation for what was to come. For those of us with doubts about the difficulty of the journey, we were reminded that the trip was to be a pilgrimage—not a vacation. Can you imagine going forty-eight hours without sleep; with two retarded children in the group? Or can you imagine traveling this distance being in your seventies or eighties, in ill health? Add to that, almost reaching your destination, being in a receiving area totally void of warmth and smiles.

The actual airport facility was very cold and drab, as were the communists, themselves. Light fixtures and furnishings were stark in appearance and shape. There was a tiny gift area which sold very plain green and brown dresses.

There were no explanations, much less apologies, for our delay. We were responsible for our own luggage. No assistance was offered.

We had no option but to patiently wait, helping each other, in love, until the official maneuvers were completed.

Why aren't we, in the United States, hearing more about Medjugorje and the phenomena of the area?

We are! I was interviewed by *USA Today* when I was in Medjugorje. *US News & World Report* magazine also did a report on Medjugorje (the issue with Ollie North's picture on the cover). There are at least six books, published in several languages, available throughout the world.

But one must be aware of the difficulty the media and others experience just getting into and out of a communist country. The communists attempt to censor everything. Much material has literally been "sneaked" out. The communists make communication very difficult.

I remember one man saying he tried to telephone out of Medjugorje for over three days! I also remember a young, innocent pilgrim who was fined and intimated by the communists, simply for carrying, and not concealing, visible religious goods.

The communists have not even permitted additional toilet facilities to accommodate the throngs of visitors.

The communists, out of fear (of a possible uprising and potential loss of control of the people), intentionally discourage visitors and attempt to squelch information about Medjugorje. Simply put, they do not want the world to know of the happenings in Medjugorje, and do everything within their power to contain it.

Can you describe an average day in Medjugorje?

The night we arrived, in spite of our exhaustion from the trip, we attended mass. These people start their day in prayer, and end it in prayer.

It was a fifteen or twenty-minute walk from Vera's home to the village church of St. James. The church was built much larger than it needed to be, long before the apparitions began. When people were asked why the church was so large, they said they didn't know, although the reason is obvious now.

Days in Medjugorje are relatively quiet, spent outdoors, with a great deal of exercise and contemplation. Our day began in line for a shower, with a prayer for hot water! If you were last, you were out of luck. After a few days it didn't even matter. Mass for the English-speaking people was at 9:00 a.m. Daily masses in several languages were available. Masses in different languages were said throughout the day.

Morning mass was followed by a group discussion and lectures outside in the fields, for our group.

Evening mass is held at 7:00. After mass, most people enjoy leisurely dinners which include discussion. Many, then, meet in prayer groups later in the evening.

What impressed you most about the area?

I was quickly and totally aware of God's brilliance. It inspired me to see sheer joy and peace in this remote corner of the communist world. Jews, Slavs, Croatian Catholics, and people who visit from all over the world have come together to help each other and coexist peacefully in the face of very rough terrain and communist adversity. We completely forgot our political, religious, and geographical extractions.

Did you ever offer to help the women of the household? If so, what was the response?

Yes, indeed I did offer to help the women of the household, realizing that Vera was up at the crack of dawn and did not retire until the wee hours of the morning. Her graciousness was very much in evidence and her home seemed to be a host home for the village, which is to say, dinner served at nine, people were still coming in at eleven or twelve at night, and Vera was still serving coffee or schnapps, or whatever anyone seemed to want, and I might add, always graciously, with love, with a smile.

If she ever experienced fatigue, you never saw it in her face. All I ever perceived in her face was peaceful joy, and I am a very observant person. In offering to help her, I was reprimanded by a Catholic nun because their joy, their love, their peace comes from serving. I was told they really are quite offended if you get up, as we would at home, or we would like our children to do, and go into the kitchen and do the dishes, or assist in any way. I carefully moved past the Catholic nun, thinking maybe with a smile and some warmth I could go into the kitchen. I felt that if everyone who was dining there at that house, that if about twenty of us pitched in, this could all be accomplished very quickly. But the mother was standing in the doorway of the kitchen as I proceeded to pass. As we were eyeball to eyeball she looked at me and said, "No . . . no . . . no . . . no . . . no." I could see great embarrassment in her face and she pointed out clearly, in some broken English, that she wanted me to sit down and enjoy my coffee. I could see that I had offended her. I still, in my own little mind, can't believe that if we all had pitched in, and established a pattern, that Vera might, after a certain period of time, enjoy having that freedom, enjoy having that time to herself, and to enjoy her family. But, it hasn't been in her experience, it hasn't been in her culture. Obviously, the women do all the housework, everything, and take pride in their day-long service. Therefore, she was not willing to accept any help.

Are the people in the village consistent in their behavior?

For *six* years buses have arrived on Saturday and left on Saturday. Millions have come to this village of approximately four hundred families, and found a home, complete with love and warmth. The average number of children in a Medjugorian home is 2.5. Elderly parents live with the families also. These people appear tireless.

Think of yourself entertaining company (whom you don't even know) daily, for over six years (over 2,000 days). Could you do it? Could you wash sheets, clean house, and cook round the clock, lovingly, for this period of time?

I ponder the statement that we will know them by their fruits.

Did staying in this remote, impoverished village change you, Ann Marie Hancock, in any specific ways?

Definitely! I was called to a total re-evaluation of my time and even my material purchases. I was once again in touch with the greatest and most precious gift of all . . . LOVE, and knowing that, indeed, we cannot put a price tag on it. I saw that true love is giving of ourselves, even when, maybe even mostly when, it's not convenient. Isn't this when we are often needed most? Is this the simple call to greatness.

These people were neither rich nor powerful, yet they had the richest and most powerful impact on my life, next to my own immediate family. These people were living examples of what we can and should be.

What was the greatest impact that your visit had on your own life?

I reassessed my own life in such a personal way, reevaluating all the things that seem so important, yet fade in the memory of the families who cooked for everyone and put their own concerns behind them. I still think about the Madonna's gentle messages to the children lovingly admonishing them for watching the time, saying we must give our hearts to God. It is so easy to lose that spiritual frame of mind. It seems we only practice, maybe one day a week, what must be lived each and every day, every minute of our lives.

I, personally, have opened my eyes to the abundant gifts and blessings in my life, which are priceless. The messages have become an integral part of my life. Each day, now, I consciously strive to live love in all facets of my life.

What has been the response of your family to your involvement in the phenomena of Medjugorje?

My immediate family is *very* loving and supportive, but as you can imagine, there have been some difficult times. Imagine a member of your family returning from a trip, telling people (including your friends) that the Mother of God is appearing in Yugoslavia.

The response from some has been that I am not "playing with a full deck!" Many people either laugh, or actually become hostile. My children, though, are strong; as is my husband. They believe me and believe in what I experienced.

How do you handle the hostility and ridicule?

It's quite easy for me because I cannot deny what I saw. I cannot deny my own experience or the experiences of millions who have journeyed to Medjugorje.

I have great compassion for hostile people. I believe many live in a state of denial, caught up in the materialism of the day. I believe many of these people are merely afraid, because suddenly, someone puts them in touch with what really matters—our spiritual well-being. Many do not want to look at themselves honestly and re-examine their values. Let's face it. This process takes genuine work, commitment, and courage.

Basically, the ridicule reminds me of how far we've drifted from our purpose, and our true selves. This is quite sad to me. But, I've learned to deal with all people, and especially the hostile ones with love and compassion.

Are many non-Catholics going to Medjugorje?

Millions of people have already visited Medjugorje, and in just the past six years. In my estimation, part of the beauty, a great part, lies in the fact that these people are from all walks of life, all religions, and from countries all over the world. I heard a Jewish woman say, "I feel at peace here."

How do people who are not Catholic respond to the events and experiences of Medjugorje?

People come from different walks of life, different countries, languages, and religions, but *all* are affected. We all are affected in different ways. Seeing thousands of people in holy mass, seeing thousands of people in the fields, and thousands of people in confession, truthfully, was the most powerful, moving, and memorable part of my journey. Seeing people from all over the world coming together in love, peace, and prayer was inspiring. I cannot comprehend anything more beautiful and powerful. Climbing up Krizevak, seeing old people and women with babies, trying to mount those grueling cliffs, and seeing different nationalities reaching out to help each other, truly touches the heart. This is what it is all about! I saw all faiths coming together in love, putting aside all bias and prejudice, and not seeing each other in any other light except as the children of God. It was extremely powerful. The Holy Mother said to take Her messages to the world; that there are no religions in Heaven. We are to live our lives as best as we can, live our lives in love and we must love everyone.

I believe we are well on our way to finding our true selves and our capacity for understanding becomes greater with each passing day. Each new day brings opportunities for hope, and love, and joy, as opposed to suffering and sorrow.

Do you feel the people who go to Medjugorje have a mission?

At the risk of sounding corny, I answer emphatically, YES. The Holy Mother has asked *each* to take her messages to the world. She has indicated that Her messages are for everyone, that we are all her children.

I certainly feel a responsibility to do so, particularly being a communicator. I believe, however, that by *living* the messages in our own lives, we become the best communicators of one of Her most important messages—love.

Other books have been written and distributed throughout the world on this topic. Why write another?

I have been asked this many times on my lecture circuit. The books written thus far have been written by Catholic clergy. While I am Catholic, myself, I am totally aware that the Holy Mother's messages are universal. She has said clearly, as the Mother of us all, that She wants to touch all Her children.

It is extremely important to me that humanity realize that these are not solely Catholic experiences and messages, but simply universal wisdom to be shared and lived by us all.

It is my hope that this book communicates this point clearly.

Why do you feel the apparitions are occurring?

Nobody would deny that these are urgent times. We live in a time when the crime rate is outrageously high, teen suicide is increasing at an alarming rate, and the threat of nuclear war looms ominously over our heads. How many of us have already forgotten Chernobyl?

The Holy Mother has come again in an attempt to help us refocus our priorities. She says we should not focus on our problems and materialism, but that we should, "Start from this moment, turn off the television, and renounce other things which are useless. Dear children, I am calling you individually to convert." (February 13, 1986, transcripts.)

When we shift our focus to love, and open our hearts, failures and tragedies are transformed into growth experiences, taking on a new meaning. With love, comes a new understanding, along with a new awareness, that everything is in divine order. Jesus has told us love is the greatest power of all. By using this power, we have the ability to change ourselves, our thoughts, and our world by simply loving; first by loving ourselves, and then by "becoming a light" and radiating that love to others. This is the only way world peace can be achieved.

Why do you feel the image of the Madonna is appearing?

As Mary has said Herself, She is the universal mother, and we are all Her children. She does not discriminate, which supports another of Her messages, that there are, indeed, no religions in Heaven. When we think of a mother, we think of love. Ponder the expression "heart of the home." A loving mother loves all her children and doesn't discriminate. Each child is special, each unique, each with his own gifts. We further associate the mother figure with kindness, gentility, guidance, and tenderness—much-needed virtues in our tired world. A mother is associated with simple tasks in the home, which, to many, would appear tedious, but are always appreciated when done in love. She is the cog that moves the family wheel. She is the catalyst that incites love in each, as Mary has come to do with Her children of our world. We need a new perspective right now—we as individuals, and we as mankind. Who is better to guide us?

Isn't it true that descriptions of the Madonna vary in different geographical locations? How do you explain this?

I see that God, in His infinite love, recognized the different cultures and the importance of communicating His messages so that they might be understood by the recipients. Is it not appropriate that in Africa She would appear black or in Croatia as a Croatian woman? It isn't the intention to frighten, but through a familiar image to communicate His love in a way that can be understood. Without understanding, it can't be lived.

Do you have any theories on why this particular parish, this particular community, was chosen as the site of the apparitions?

I think the Madonna is trying to demonstrate what can be accomplished on a universal level, by using Medjugorje as a microcosm of the world, as it were. There are many differentiations in the culture and politics of Medjugorje: the Serbs, the Turks, the Muslims, the Jewish people, the Croatian Catholics, all coexist in this small village. It was a village of major conflict, and a troubled area, as well as a communist village. The Madonna is wise beyond my expression, or my ability to express Her wisdom, in that She chose a remote area where She brought people together from all over the world. How magnificent! If She could bring that whole village together, to coexist peacefully together, how beautiful. If She can inspire young people and teenagers to return to God, in these troubled times, when there are many who even question the validity of God, how wonderful!

Has She not made Her messages to the world clear? If we can do it there, we can do it anywhere, but only if we exercise our intellect, our hearts, and our free wills to love, to choose love, as opposed to hatred, bitterness, fear, and most of all, judgment. When we point a finger at another, we are basically fearful of our own self-image, and at some level, trying to enhance our own image by criticizing another. When, subconsciously we know where the real problem is, and as long as we are pointing fingers, we cannot change. Unless we are without sin, we must learn not to cast stones! Until we can look at every person with love, until we can accept and respect every human being as a child of God, we still have inner work to do.

If the people of the world became aware of the apparitions and accepted the messages as truth, do you perceive this phenomena creating a weakness with existing religious organizations or possibly even creating a new religious movement?

I think it is important to understand that even in the Catholic faith, Mary is not meant to be adored. Rather, as Jesus' Mother, She is an intercessor between God and His children. Historically, the Lord has sent Her in times of peril and urgency, as in Fatima, preceding World War I. Mary, Herself, has said in Medjugorje that She is not the one who heals. It is God. She always defers to God, to the Lord. I think this is extremely important. She is clearly the intercessor, as I might be for my husband, relaying a message from him, to a member of my family.

The messages shared by the Holy Mother are universal in nature. They transcend all religion and faiths, as many spiritual writings do. If we can only release our egotistical, human limitations, and open our hearts to Her message, as She has requested many times, we will understand. She has come to unite us all in Christ, not separate us further from each other.

Hopefully, we as a world of many religions, will see with our hearts, the common Truth in what the Madonna speaks. As we open our hearts, we may see more similarities than differences in various religions. This, itself, will strengthen each person's faith. We are all on this earth together. The issue is not a mater of religion, but of unity, and peaceful coexistence. Knowing this, how can the apparitions create any weakness within existing religions. The messages are simple, and so universal. If any weakness is created, it will be rooted in human minds, stemming from a lack of understanding.

Ann Marie, why do you feel the apparitions are revealed to children?

Children are generally honest and open. They, in their purest form, are uninhibited receptacles of love. Instead of trying to change our children, we can often learn much from them, as, they too, are our teachers.

I think it is sad that often, as we grow older, we lose this receptivity. As adults, we tend to be so busy doing, that we don't take the time just to be ourselves. We learn to doubt, rather than express our faith. We become preoccupied with what other people think. Our capacity to love and be open, once uninhibited, becomes tainted by anger, fear, daily concerns, and other forms of social conditioning.

Children, on the other hand, live for the moment. I remember Christ's words: "I tell you solemnly, unless you change and become like little children you will never enter the kingdom of heaven. And so, the one who makes himself as little as this little child is the greatest in the kingdom of heaven." (Matt. 18:3)

In Medjugorje, there are six children, all with divergent personalities, saying the same thing, over a long period of time, never deviating, every day for six years. Maybe someone could lie for one year, but for six years? That's a long time. And six years to pray four hours a day? Could you do that? These six youths do, daily. God is trying to stir souls. He is trying to move hearts. He is trying to open hearts, through these six children, these youthful examples of what we, too, can become.

Could you share some detailed impressions of the visionaries?

The visionaries have had to be protected from the crowds. Many people desire to touch them, and have tugged at their clothing. Since I was allowed into the room of apparitions (a priest's bedroom in St. James church where the visionaries generally receive the apparitions), I was able to observe them at a close distance. Only Marija and Jakov were present that day. Vicka was receiving the apparitions in her home, as often she is too ill to go to the rectory.

I first saw Marija and Jakov clearly when I knelt behind them, and to the side, in the room of apparitions. I was intent on watching their faces, since a priest from Ireland had already told me, at dinner the night before, that their reverence and devotion was so moving. I wanted to see for myself.

Marija's clothing first caught me eye. She wore a red sweater, a skirt, and knee socks. Her hair is relatively short and dark. Her dark eyes danced. She could be anybody's teenage daughter (although she is now twenty-one!).

I was surprised when a restless child in the room cried out, and Marija turned around to smile and touch her. The child stopped crying immediately.

I had a preconceived mental picture of Jakov which I had formed from one of the books I had read. I envisioned a small, mischievous ten-year-old boy. I was amazed at the stature of this sixteen-year-old. He is tall and very attractive. He wore slacks and a dark sweater. He gave the appearance of being very calm and very much at "peace." As I remember him, Jakov, too, had dark eyes and a crop of hair on the darker side, and typical of today's college set. He, too, appeared very typical. I did not see the mischievousness in his eyes that is mentioned in many books.

The two began by literally squeezing into the crowded room, quietly and unobtrusively, almost without being noticed. Then they began, with an indescribable reverence, praying the rosary in Croatian. They seemed to be in a world of their own. One could watch their faces forever. While not the faces of movie stars, their beauty was awe-inspiring; a beauty that radiated as a light from within their beings, but also a light that seemed to touch every heart in the room. After the recitation of the rosary, simultaneously, the two moved to the center of the room. There they stood for a moment, then dropped to their knees in total synchronicity, while making the sign of the cross. Their eyes were riveted upwards, in an almost fixed position. Their lips moved, but no sounds emerged.

I will never forget the experience. I looked away from them at my own rosary beads in my hands, and my rosary seemed to radiate pink lights from every bead. I could feel tears filling my eyes, and a joy I could never describe. Words are insufficient.

The children left the room quickly, when the apparition ceased. I noticed their patience with the crowds in the hallway leading to the room. I noticed their warmth and extreme sense of courtesy. Everyone wanted to touch them or speak to them. Yet, the two seemed so humbly balanced, and always polite.

Do you know anything specific about their personalities that renders them funny or witty?

There are many stories, but one specific incident I recall was told by a tour guide who visits Medjugorje regularly. The gentleman helps with crowd control outside the room of apparitions (remember people start gathering early in the morning in hopes of getting in).

One particular day Marija was working her way through the crowds and up the stairs of the rectory when this tour guide inadvertently stopped her. She laughed, as though she was going to pull out some identification and said, "I'm Marija, visionary!" They both chuckled, as she continued on.

The children are all loved for their warmth and keen wits.

What about Jakov?

When the apparitions began, Jakov, the youngest (only ten) became the greatest target for inquiries about the secrets. There were those who thought that if there was a secret to be revealed, the youngest would be the most likely candidate to "spill the beans." Jakov, though, was quick to indicate that he felt the secrets were safest in his possession. He was not one to be tempted. I was told that Jakov was always gracious, and could match any adult's keen wit or attempts at trickery.

Did you see Vicka?

Yes, more than once. I passed her Easter Sunday in the church as she moved through the crowds, radiating one of the warmest smiles I'd ever seen. I observed an incredible strength and determination in her face. Also, one night, quite late in the evening, I walked to the hill of apparitions. I saw Vicka with two friends praying at the foot of the cross.

Vicka also makes herself accessible to visiting pilgrims. Daily, in the courtyard of her home, she visits with others. Going from Vera's home to the hill of apparitions, I passed Vicka's house. I remember seeing her daily answering questions and visiting with pilgrims.

According to the records of the apparitions in Lourdes and Fatima, and the accounts of Medjugorje, a light precedes the apparitions. How do you explain this?

I suppose that I have not gone so far in my thinking as to analyze, dissect, and rationalize what those lights are. I think we often get into trouble by trying to analyze phenomena, and dissect it. We reduce it. Then we have great difficulty comprehending the meaning of its isolated fragments. We rarely see the forest when we focus on isolated trees. How often do we miss "the big picture?"

I perceive the light as supernatural phenomena, as obvious signs from God, to get our attention; just as a light goes on in a room, a light comes on in our hearts, or the lights going on in the streets. It's a wonderful way to get our attention. Now the physicists (and I will leave it to the physicists) have many incredible descriptions, employing all the ninety-cent words that I can't comprehend. Basically, though, they are explaining the light as a very powerful pure energy. I find that very interesting in terms of my own rosary beads in the room of apparitions. I saw the pink lights, and the chain had turned from silver to gold. Someone commented to me that the powerful love energy in that room interacted with the chemicals or acid in the body. But that's not important, it got my attention!

Was it difficult for you, being Catholic, and writing a book about Medjugorje when the apparitions have not yet been approved by the Church?
Absolutely not, I had no difficulty with this whatsoever. Of course, the Church's stance on apparitions is an unusual one anyway. Catholics are not obliged to believe in apparitions, though investigating. At this time, the church is not recognizing these apparitions. Historically, it has taken thirteen years for the church to recognize this type of divine phenomena (i.e. Lourdes, Fatima).

After having been to Medjugorje, I cannot deny what I have seen. I cannot deny what I have experienced. I am not just talking specifically about signs and wonders such as crosses spinning and the Miracle of the Sun. What I am talking about, and of primary importance to me, are the accomplishments, the achievements that have been made through the messages of Mary. I have seen people of all political extractions come together, and I have seen people of all religions come together, in love, and in joy. I have seen people truly and selflessly giving of themselves. I observed a German, a Dutchman, and a Frenchman, all assisting an old woman. They were all climbing a hill together, while passing the woman among them. It was very, very moving to see this kind of thing, and to know that historically, this area had been ridden with strife, previous to the apparitions. Now, Muslims, Slavs, Jews, Serbs, and Croatians all live peacefully together. It was an overwhelming feeling to see this accomplishment, something that we, as people, rarely achieve ourselves. I can never deny what is in my own experience. I can never deny the peace that comes from being witness to total transformation. It's as if Mary, or I should say God, in His grand design, chose Medjugorje to demonstrate a microcosm of the world, of ourselves, and what we can become.

As a Catholic, how will the Church's final position on the authenticity of the apparitions affect your beliefs and experience?
First of all, the Church does not insist that we accept apparitions. I

suppose in my own mind I have a little trouble with the lengthy validation process; only from the standpoint that the Mother of God is telling us that we're almost out of time. Urgency is constantly emphasized. We know there are three chastisements. The Madonna specifically says that they are coming soon, and that She has stayed too long. She has even said that there will be time between the first and second chastisements to convert, but after that, there will to *no* time. I have some difficulty negotiating the Church's thirteen-year investigative process, in light of these messages. I think we need guidance desperately. The Madonna, Herself, has clearly asked us to take Her messages to the world, and told us of the urgency. We don't have thirteen years! I believe the Madonna's words. I believe we're on a self-destructive course. We are almost out of time. I feel that urgency to share the messages, and I am doing exactly that!

Are people coming to Medjugorje expecting a miracle, a healing?

Of course there are those journeying to Medjugorje with those expectations. In all holy places, those desiring miracles or healings can be found. Some are healed immediately, some, in time, as with little Daniel, and some may have to change attitudes, belief and value systems before any healing *can* occur. Most of the people I met did not come for healings. They came to see, and experience this very special place. They take home much more, I'm sure, than anyone can even anticipate. For, it was like being in the presence of God, a true heaven on earth. It's truly indescribable, but definitely an experience I will carry with me, and draw from, always.

If no healing takes place, and in fact death occurs, how do you explain the "absence of a miracle?"

I know of no deaths occurring in Medjugorje, in which the "absence of a miracle" was cited as the cause. I have no definite explanation for this question, I can only surmise. The Holy Mother emphasizes that faith is essential for healing. It has been proven that one's state of mind affects (probably to a greater degree than we realize) one's physical well-being. As in Vicka's case, with her brain cyst, she prays that God's will, and not hers be done. She has faith that all is in Divine order. Her complete faith, again, is an example of what *we* must strive for. Do we really know what's best for us? Maybe, if we saw a physical ailment as a symptom of a deeper challenge, we might be able to accept and understand it better. I believe illnesses are often symptoms of something askew in our lives, which usually stems from inhibiting thoughts, deeds, or actions. These are what we must look at.

Couldn't it be possible, if we resent a personal illness enough, and live negatively, that we might kill ourselves, through destructive emotions such as anger and resentment, along with their related mental anguish? Plus, what if someone dies? Who are *we* to judge what is best for that soul's development? Death, too, is a blessing! That's a "heavy" statement; ponder it.

Did you personally experience the Miracle of the Sun?

The Tuesday evening I came out of the room of apparitions, I noticed groups of people staring at the sky. When Jackie Bailey and I looked up, we compared notes. There appeared to be disc-like colors becoming larger and larger around the sun. Then, quickly, those were replaced by brighter and deeper colors. We both noticed a long ridge of deep purple across the mountain where the cross of Krizevak stands. Then, the ridge turned pink, and again changed—this time to bright yellow.

Jackie and I also saw the cross spinning. First, we saw the cross bar, and then we didn't! To my amazement, we both experienced the same visual perceptions.

What about those who see Mary on a cloud?

Many have experienced this. Jackie Bailey spoke to a Catholic nun from New York who had seen Mary on a cloud. Jackie said that the nun was ecstatic. Non-Catholics have also reported seeing Her on a cloud. While I was there, a group from Belgium witnessed this phenomenon, too.

What wonders affected you most?

I remember our two-hour climb up the rocky cliffs to Mt. Krizevak, seeing people of all nations saying the stations of the cross. I recall hearing at least five different languages. I can still see, in my mind, one very fragile old woman, probably in her eighties, wearing a kerchief and a modest black coat. She was speaking in a foreign tongue, I thought to be German. The old woman had great difficulty walking. An Italian gentleman helped her for a distance, then carefully handed her to a Dutchman. The Americans pitched in and a French group also assisted her. As I observed this, great emotion surged within me. I heard only "please" and "thank you" in the different languages, as I saw the smiling faces radiating and *living* this unconditional love.

The old woman was kneeling at the foot of the cross when our group reached the top. The air on top was bitter cold as the wind pushed against us. I wonder if this old woman had brought a lunch, as the climb down would probably take another two hours. When I got close enough to see her face, I saw that it didn't matter. There were tears flowing from her eyes, and a peace in her face, that lunch or no lunch, could replace. I won't forget her.

What are your personal reactions to the phenomena occurring in Medjugorje?

In my personal attempt to grasp the big picture, I have often wondered, during all of this, if God isn't sitting up there, perched out on a limb somewhere, looking down saying, "Okay, I've sent my Son, I've sent His Mother . . . *What's left?* If that might be the case, my response, my reaction is that it's time to respond. I think that's His message. It's time to do it. It's time to *be* it. It's time to *live* it.

What do you feel is the content or nature of the ten secrets and chastisements?

I do not have any idea of the specific information contained in the secrets. I do believe that we live in times where we have created problems through our technology, and have completely lost our focus on priorities. Those priorities being: accepting responsibility for each individual self, and not handing that to a counselor, or therapist. I'm not saying there is no need for these services, but I am saying that, perhaps, if we focus on our personal friendship with Jesus, and live these messages, we will become more in touch with ourselves, and become better examples for the rest of the world.

Do you feel there will be more signs and wonders in Medjugorje, or anywhere else in the world?

We constantly have signs, but few of us related them to "the big picture." Erratic weather, earthquakes, volcanos, and tidal waves are now occurring with greater frequency than ever before. These are all physical signs. Increasing mental confusion, resulting in suicides, drug and alcohol problems, insanity, and other illnesses are also signs of our times.

Yes, there will be more signs in Medjugorje, at least one. The Holy Mother has told us of the "greatest sign of all" which will be left at the first site of the apparitions, on Mt. Podbrdo. We are living in very exciting times. We must not fear these signs. We can choose to accept the Madonna's messages and live them. If we do this, we can look forward to our future, with great anticipation of what our world will transform into.

What is the reaction to signs and wonders?

I think it's a personal thing. I remember walking to the church with two teenage boys from New Orleans who were very open and honest. They said, at first, they didn't want to come, but their parents made them. They quickly added, though, that they were so happy they came, that they couldn't wait to go home and share the messages with their friends. I asked them if they were concerned about their friend's reactions. They both said "no"; adding that each had found strength and peace in Medjugorje that changed their lives. I asked them if they had seen the Miracle of the Sun. They had, but said it didn't matter, that what was important was all these people coming together from everywhere in love. Both were visibly moved.

I interviewed a dentist from New Orleans who dabbled in farming. He explained the crops growing in the fields to me. To my surprise, he said the same thing the teenage boys had said to me. The love he felt in Medjugorje overwhelmed him, and had changed his life.

Many I talked to went to Medjugorje for one reason—the peace. I was amazed at the number of individuals I personally interviewed there who said, "Yes, I saw the Miracle of the Sun. Yes, I saw the Cross spin at Krizevak. Yes, I saw Mary on a cloud. But do you know the most beautiful thing is seeing thousands from all over the world, in this one place, in this small impoverished village, coming together in love. If you need the signs, they're available." It was very interesting that most of the people I spoke with were not preoccupied with these beautiful wonders that God made available to them. Rather, they were captivated by the love and the peace that they felt as they all stood together in love.

How do you feel about people making pilgrimages to other holy world locations such as Jerusalem, or the Great Wall of China?

I think that everyone should have the option to choose where each finds his own peace. I think it's extremely important that, at some point in time, we do what we need to do to trigger that consciousness in us that takes us back on the path to God. If it's the Great Wall, then I think that's significant. If it's Jerusalem, I think that's significant. It's an individual thing. No one can answer that question for another person.

The only danger that I perceive is the possibility of isolating the one experience. For instance, in the case of Medjugorje, one might think that's all there is, nothing else exists, and we just hang on to all the phenomena associated with Medjugorje. Then, I think one is in danger of losing one's perspective. We need to take the messages and incorporate them into our own experiences. Then take the experiences, move them into our hearts, give them a proper perspective, using love, and simply allow for more experience, based on love. As we continue to integrate our experiences in the language of our hearts, we come to realize that the holiest places are in the heart.

You believe that the apparitions are calling everyone to God, and not just the Catholics?

Yes, and I will say this, the word Catholic, from its Greek origin, via translation, means universal. I feel the Holy Mother is calling us universally back to God. I will also add that she has said clearly that we are all her children. I think this comment is extremely pertinent, and demonstrates the transcendent nature of her messages. I think we are all being called to be Christ-like, whether Catholic, Lutheran, or Buddhist.

Is the Holy Mother calling us to Catholic prayer?

Mary does not dictate the way we should pray. Of primary importance is that we pray with our hearts, with surrender, and without attention given to our clocks and watches. She lovingly reprimanded the visionaries, and the members of the parish prayer group, for watching their clocks. She stressed the importance of giving ourselves to God and with this action, that we would be provided for. Those who were reprimanded discovered that when opening their hearts in prayer, ample time for everything else followed.

What significance do you place on the Madonna's request for fasting?

Many of the worlds' religions include fasting in their practices. I think too many people get caught up in the martyr/suffering aspect of fasting, though. I, personally, perceive physical fasting as a detoxification process, a process of cleansing. I believe with this physical purification process, the body can better function as an integral unit, thus, increasing the ability to communicate with, and receive assistance from God. By removing toxins and chemicals that may interfere with our receptivity, we become more open and receptive vessels of God's love and wisdom. For me, it is an act of cleansing and preparing the body for a higher awareness of God. I like to think of my body as a temple in which personal holiness can be developed. If we defile our bodies, in any way, how can we expect to fulfill our potential? Fasting serves as a tool, and aid to our friendship with Christ.

The call to fasting seems ancient and maybe a bit extreme, don't you think?

Absolutely not! Fasting has been with us since the beginning of time. It is a discipline that signifies commitment, commitment to better ourselves.

Fasting, as explained to me in Medjugorje, does not always mean physical fasting on bread and water. It means de-emphasizing something material that has meaning for us—to replace it with a spiritual commitment. If it's television, then maybe we could sacrifice a favorite show. If it's cigarettes, which are harmful to the body (the temple of the soul), one could start by cutting back, and then, eventually quitting.

Mary has explained that She is not calling us to extraordinary things, but to lead simple lives in love and fulfillment of commitments.

Do you think when the Holy Mother calls us to confession, that she is referring to the Catholic Sacrament of Penance?

I, as a Catholic, see the priest as a representative of Christ of earth. When we truly examine our consciences, we recognize what we have done; those things which we feel are less than acceptable. We definitely feel we must make amends for those things. The Catholic Church has provided for atonement of these mistakes, the Sacrament of Confession. Again, as with the message of conversion, it would be unfortunate for the universality of the "confession" message to be lost in specifically religious interpretation. Acknowledging what one perceives to be their failure and mistakes is essential. The atonement must take place within one's heart, and with God. This intimate connection requires the language of its own honesty, purity, and love.

Does this mean that Catholics have no need of the Sacrament of Confession? *Certainly not,* but it does allow those non-Catholics the forgiveness and love from God that Mary, through the simplicity of her messages, is bringing to all people.

Do you feel one has to be Catholic to be "saved"?

Absolutely not! The Catholic way works for me and for my family. But I believe we each find our own path to God, and that there are many paths. I feel that it is very narrow-minded and somewhat judgmental to think any one of us, has the only answer, or exclusive knowledge of the will and wisdom of the Father. Why can't we permit each other to journey our own paths to God, with love and acceptance; even if the paths are different? Are we so threatened? If so maybe we need to look closer at ourselves.

It almost amuses me that anyone could be so arrogant as to think that God only hears and answers select prayers. He loves *all* who live their lives for Him and in Him. I believe this with my whole heart and soul.

When Ivanka, the visionary, asked the Holy Mother about her deceased mother, who was not devoutly religious, but a good woman and mother, the Madonna replied that Ivanka's earthly mother was with Her. Later, Ivanka saw her earthly mother with the Madonna. This example seems to show that one doesn't have to be devoutly religious to experience the kingdom of God.

You mentioned that humility was one of the key messages, but said no more. Is humility, in fact, important?

Yes, indeed! Humility is an integral part of the transforming experience. This, again, is a matter of semantics, though. I believe the humility the Holy Mother speaks about encompasses a submissiveness, a deference to God and God's will, versus our own. Once we acknowledge our friendship with God and His unconditional love, we gain a greater understanding of our worth and our value to others. This evolves into a knowingness that *we* are not performing great acts of love, or charity, etc., but that God is working through us, and that we are, in fact, *living* our potential, our light, at these times. As this increases, the need to bolster our fragile egos diminishes. Pretentiousness, pride, and arrogance feed our egos. When we realign our priorities, we no longer need to feed the ego, as the core, the soul, is nurtured spiritually. Egotistical characteristics fall to the wayside as inner humility is developed. Quiet actions replace unending verbiage.

Do you feel there is any danger that the apparitions are becoming the focal point in Medjugorje, jeopardizing the significance of the messages?

Some people are intrigued with phenomena. The phenomena are occurring to get our attention. But phenomena cannot hold our hearts. The messages can, and do. Again, the Madonna has come with urgent messages, delivering them lovingly, in a time of peril. Take these messages, use them, incorporate them in your lives. If this is not done, any other focus is immaterial. Get past the events and *live* the messages. We can *all* do that within the framework of our own personal faiths and existing religions.

What do you feel people in general gain by making the pilgrimage to Medjugorje?

I would hope that most pilgrims to Medjugorje carry home with them a heightened awareness and awakened consciousness of unity, of love, and of peace, as I did. I can only describe the impression Medjugorje left within me. People come from different walks of life, different countries, languages, religions, but *all* have to be affected by the enveloping air of love. To see these thousands of people in holy mass, to see thousands of people in the fields, and thousands of people in confession, in this little village, is a very moving experience. Truthfully, the most powerful, moving, and memorable part of my journey was seeing people from all over the world uniting together in love, peace, and prayer. I cannot comprehend anything more beautiful or powerful.

The climb up Krizevak was also very moving. I saw old people and women with babies, trying to mount the grueling cliffs. I observed several people, of many different nationalities, reaching out to help others with the climb. This truly touched my heart. This is what Medjugorje is all about, seeing all the nationalities, and all the faiths coming together. All bias and prejudice were set aside. People saw each other only as children of God, working together. It was extremely powerful, more impressive than I can even describe.

The Madonna has said to take Her messages to the world and that there are no religions in heaven. The people in Medjugorje have realized that we are all children of God. We must live our lives as best we can—live our lives in love. We must love *everyone*. Being witness to Medjugorje, I believe we are well on our way to finding our true selves. I know there are others who feel the same way. I personally know of several others whose experiences were so profound, that they are now devoting their lives to spreading the Madonna's universal messages, and, of greater significance, living them. I truly believe, through unconditional love, all things are possible.

What have you observed in sharing the messages since you've arrived back in the states?

For the most part, it has been surprising. I go somewhere *thinking* I'll be talking to twenty-five people, and I end up with 150 people. Some even travel great distances to hear me. Then someone tells someone else, and I'm speaking a week later, and so on, and so on.

My background and knowledge of speech tell me that people become quite bored after about thirty minutes of lecturing. The fact remains that I spoke at a dinner scheduled for 7:30 p.m. and people were still asking questions shortly before midnight! I have yet to leave a speaking engagement in less than three hours. It is obvious, to me, that the Holy Mother is, Herself, at work.

If you had to summarize the messages that the Holy Mother has been sharing for six years, what would you say?

Mary's message is a call back to God—a call back to her Son—in a world consumed with power and materialism. Her message is not a new one, but one that has been with us since time immemorial, to love our neighbors as ourselves, with God as the focal point of our lives.

We do not need to attend seminars, nor do we need to study books or travel to find God. We need to unlock our hearts and find the wellspring of love that is there waiting within each of us.

What if the apparitions are a hoax, or an illusion, or merely a figment of the children's imagination?

I think it is sad that in the evolution of our highly scientific and technological culture, mystical phenomena have been degraded, and indeed, have been reduced and categorized into a realm that often frightens or humors people. Will we continue to deny the testing of the children, the weeping statutes that have been reported, witnessed and photographed in Japan, Canada, China, Pittsburgh, and other places?

Does it really matter? If we learn to love, if we return our lives to God, it's rather immaterial, because the essence of the information being given in Medjugorje is a lesson for all of us. It is not something that is merely being talked about, as so many religious "happenings" are. It is being lived and expressed every day. The transformation in what used to be a divided and unstable community, to one where some communists, themselves, have become part of the experience, is beautiful. I suppose, when all is said and done, each person must ask themselves if this is something they can accept. It becomes, once again, a matter of the heart, which truly is where the choice must be made.

Perhaps, the best response to the "what if" question of hoax or illusion is reflected in a comment made by a visitor to Medjugorje: "At Medjugorje I did not see the face of the Virgin, but I saw her reflection in the face of the people there. I do not know if Our Lady appeared to the young people, but I see that she has appeared to the world." (*Is the Virgin Mary Appearing at Medjugorje?*, page 136.)

You say be a light, but I'm only one person. Surely, you can't hope to change everybody?

Yes, I can hope, I can pray. I believe, as we have been told by the Madonna, that the laws of nature can be suspended through prayer. I can't afford to take a defeatist attitude nor can you. What good does it do?

Think of the lives you touch in the course of the day, most important, your own family, a small microcosm of the universe. But don't forget the man in the toll booth, the clerk in the store, the people in the office, the restaurant where you lunch, etc., etc. Love and patience are unmistakable, as is a smile. Begin from within, now, and give the rest to God. We, *each* of us, can touch hearts, we can make a difference.

You make everything sound so simple. Can life really be that simple?

Most definitely yes! We, often are victims of our egos. I have heard that ego means "easing God out." We use our intellects to make simple matters complex, simple decisions confusing, and simple explanations complicated. Professionals and scientists use ninety-cent words to describe very simple concepts. We all do it sometimes, to bolster our self-worth, but it really isn't necessary at all. Once we truly find Christ, we no longer need our egos. Life is meant to be simple! We are the ones who complicate things. There is a beauty in simplicity. It cuts through all the garbage. That's what we must do too. Making the connection with God, accepting the source, allowing Him to guide us, and living love, joy, and peace. It *is* simple.

The Madonna is not making demands. She loves us all "even when we are far away." Perhaps she is saying use your intellect, use your hearts, use your free wills, be the best you can be, don't let others decide for you, make your own choices? It really is simple, but to know this simplicity, one must choose to *be a light!*

Appendix II

For more information, you can write:

FRANCISCAN UNIVERSITY PRESS
UNIVERSITY OF STEUBENVILLE
STEUBENVILLE, OHIO 43952
Distributes:
  -Books
  -Video and Audio Cassettes
  -Transcripts of Holy Mother's Thursday Night Messages
  -Special Medjugorje Prints
Phone orders only:
  1-800-282-8283
  1-614-283-3771 (in Ohio)

THE CENTER FOR PEACE
P.O. BOX 66
ESSEX STREET STATION
BOSTON, MASSACHUSETTS 02112
Distributes: Updated Information
  -Books
  -Video Tapes
Arranges Tours to Medjugorje

MEDJUGORJE CENTER
C/O MARKET SQUARE SHOPPING CENTER
1450 S. 25TH STREET
FARGO, NORTH DAKOTA 58103
Distributes:
  -Newsletter (Miracle at Medjugorje)

THE MARIAN MOVEMENT OF PRIESTS
NATIONAL HEADQUARTERS
P.O. BOX 8
ST. FRANCIS, MAINE 04774-0008

Distributes:
 -Transcripts of Messages Received by Priests
 -Book (Our Lady Speaks To Her Beloved Priests)

GLOBAL TOURS, INC.
P.O. BOX 1215
PICAYUNE, MISSISSIPPI 39466
(601) 798-7359
Arranges Tours to Medjugorje

Resources

The Holy Bible/New Catholic Edition, 1957

Kraljevic, Father Svetozar. *The Apparitions of Our Lady of Medjugorje*. Chicago: Franciscan Herald Press, 1984.

Laurentin, Rene, and Rupcic, Ljudevik. *Is the Virgin Mary Appearing at Medjugorje?* The Word Among Us Press, 1984.

Pelletier A. A., Joseph A. *The Queen of Peace Visits Medjugorje*. Worcester, Ma.: An Assumption Publication, 1985.

Pervan O. F. M., Tomislav. *Queen of Peace, Echo of the Eternal Word*. Steubenville, Oh.: Franciscan University Press, 1986.

Rooney SND, Lucy and Faricy SJ, Robert. *Medjugorje Unfolds, Mary Speaks to the World*. Cork, Ireland: The Mercier Press Limited, 1985.

Rupcic O.F.M., Dr. Ljudevik. *Gospina Ukazana U Medjugorje (the Apparitions of Our Lady at Medjugorje)*. Tisak: "A. G. Matos," Samobor, 1983.

Transcripts (of messages received by priests). St. Francis, Ma.: The Marian Movement of Priests, 1987.

Transcripts (of Thursday Night Public Messages). Steubenville, Ohio: Franciscan University Press, 1987.

Weible, Wayne. "Miracle at Medjugorje." July, 1987.